TAKEN
by the
MOBSTER
MIMI FRANCIS

MASSACHUSETTS MAFIA 1

TAKEN
by the
MOBSTER

MIMI FRANCIS

4 Horsemen
Publications, Inc.

Taken by the Mobster
Copyright © 2023 Mimi Francis. All rights reserved.

4 Horsemen Publications, Inc.
1497 Main St. Suite 169
Dunedin, FL 34698
4horsemenpublications.com
info@4horsemenpublications.com

Cover by Niki Tantillo
Typesetting by Autumn Skye
Edited by Blair Parke

All rights to the work within are reserved to the author and publisher. No part of this publication may be reproduced, stored in a retrieval system, or transmitted in any form or by any means, electronic, mechanical, photocopying, recording, scanning, or otherwise, except as permitted under Section 107 or 108 of the 1976 International Copyright Act, without prior written permission except in brief quotations embodied in critical articles and reviews. Please contact either the Publisher or Author to gain permission.

This is a work of fiction. All characters, organizations, and events portrayed in this novel are either products of the author's imagination or are used fictitiously.

Library of Congress Control Number: 2023945214

Paperback ISBN-13: 979-8-8232-0308-1
Hardcover ISBN-13: 979-8-8232-0309-8
Audiobook ISBN-13: 979-8-8232-0307-4
Ebook ISBN-13: 979-8-8232-0310-4

Dedication

For my dark romance trope-loving eldest daughter, Ariana: I love talking books with you and getting excited about authors. I love it when you tell me, "Mommy, you should write an [insert trope here] book." You give me all the good ideas, and I hope someday I can write them all. I love you!

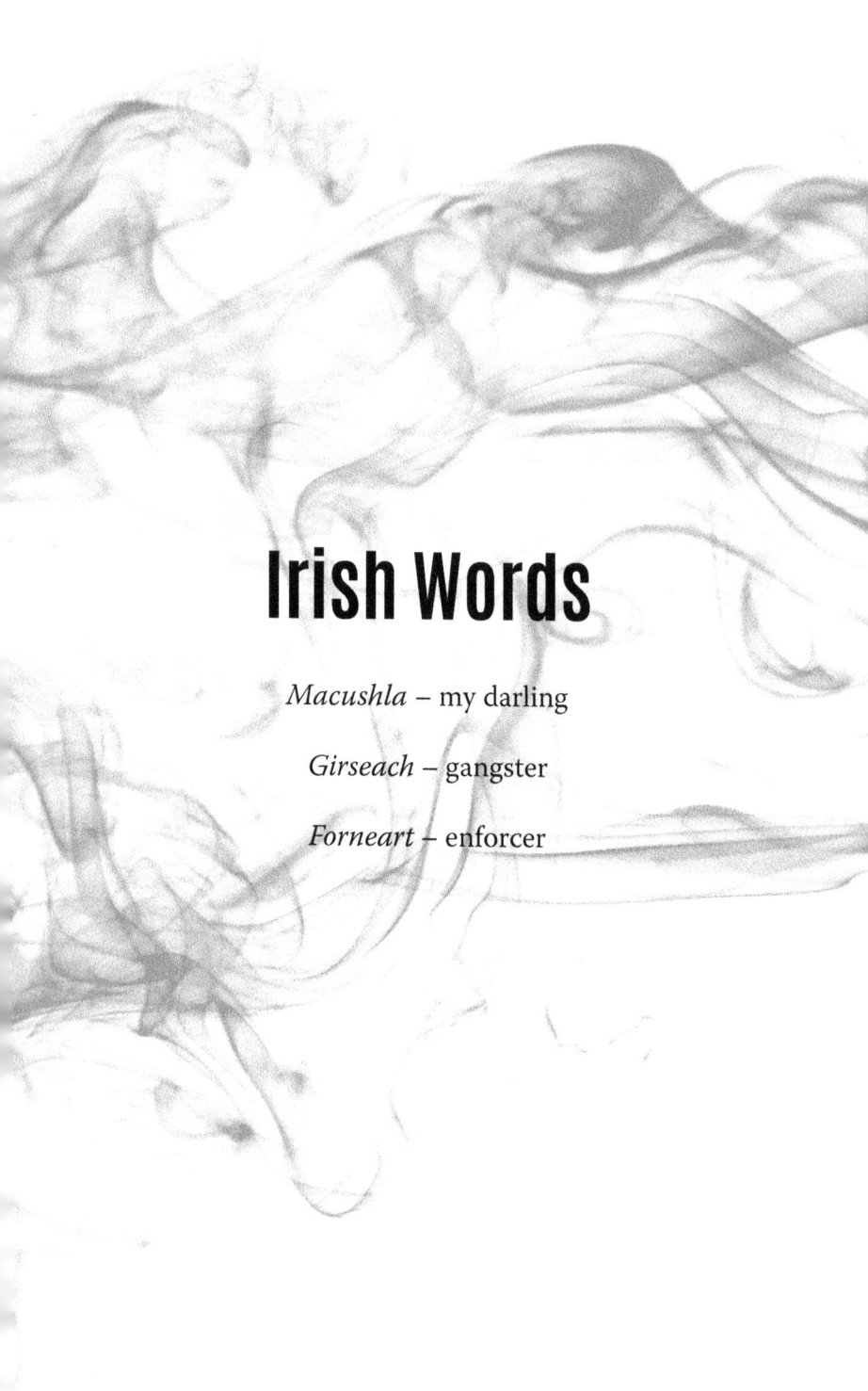

Irish Words

Macushla – my darling

Girseach – gangster

Forneart – enforcer

Contents

CHAPTER 1.....................................1
CHAPTER 2.....................................9
CHAPTER 3....................................16
CHAPTER 4....................................23
CHAPTER 5....................................31
CHAPTER 6....................................38
CHAPTER 7....................................47
CHAPTER 8....................................57
CHAPTER 9....................................64
CHAPTER 10...................................72
CHAPTER 11...................................81
CHAPTER 12...................................87
CHAPTER 13...................................95
CHAPTER 14..................................100
CHAPTER 15..................................108
CHAPTER 16..................................115
CHAPTER 17..................................121
CHAPTER 18..................................128
CHAPTER 19..................................134
CHAPTER 20..................................142
CHAPTER 21..................................151
CHAPTER 22..................................160
CHAPTER 23..................................169

CHAPTER 24..................................176
CHAPTER 25..................................183
CHAPTER 26..................................190
CHAPTER 27..................................198
CHAPTER 28..................................203
CHAPTER 29..................................211
CHAPTER 30..................................218

BOOK CLUB QUESTIONS 225
SNEAK PEAK AT BOOK 2 227
AUTHOR BIO 243

Chapter 1
Olivia

Olivia checked the clock on the wall for the fifth time; fifteen minutes until the bank closed its doors for the day. Whenever the door opened, the sounds of the outside world invaded the bank, and the crisp, clean, cold air from outside swirled through the room. She pushed her dark brown hair behind her ear with one finger and looked around the dimly lit bank. There were only a few customers left. Most of them were the usual closing time customers; it wouldn't take long to help them with their transactions.

Her boss, Mr. Ingalls, walked by with a slight frown, tapped the face of his watch, and twirled his finger at Olivia in a move-it-along gesture. He was eager to close the bank. Ever since his wife became ill, the day couldn't end soon enough for him; she was his priority.

Olivia would have preferred to stay, if only to avoid another night alone in her shitty motel room, mourning the loss of her life and the family she loved. Not that the motel was home. Home was Massachusetts, and she couldn't go back there right now or ever.

The tiny bell over the door chimed, signaling the arrival of another customer. The owner of the gas station across the street, one of her regulars, came in to make his daily deposit. A rush of cold fall air followed him inside, making her shiver. She saw the shadows from nearby buildings stretching out into the street, growing noticeably longer as night encroached. Olivia straightened her shoulders and put on her best smile for her customer.

"Good evening, Mr. Sewell." Her own voice sounded falsely bright to her ears. Mr. Sewell didn't seem to notice.

"Billy, please, Mrs. Miller," he scolded. "Please call me Billy."

Olivia nodded and smiled. She made quick work of his daily deposit; he would be eager to get home. It was one transaction she didn't take her time doing. Mr. Sewell smiled and winked at her before scurrying out the door with purposeful intent, perhaps hurrying home to his wife and young daughter. Olivia felt a pang of jealousy that he got to see his family.

The click of the key turning in the lock on the bank doors made her heart ache with loneliness. She refrained from sighing and focused on counting her cash drawer before securing it in the safe. She walked with her boss to the back door where Olivia put on her jacket and blue scarf while listening to Mr. Ingalls, nodding in all the appropriate places while already dreading her lonely evening.

"You're sure you'll be all right with closing next week?" Mr. Ingalls inquired, as he held the back exit door open for her. "I understand it's a lot to ask—."

"I'll be fine, Mr. Ingalls." Olivia slipped on her gloves before stepping outside. "It's the least I can do. Margaret will be happy to have you home early. Please don't worry. I'm happy to help."

Mr. Ingalls squeezed her arm. "What would I do without you, Olivia? Thank you for everything."

Chapter 1

They said their goodbyes for the evening. Olivia turned to walk the short distance to the motel, only a few blocks from the bank. Despite the cold, she took her time; she was in no hurry to lock herself in her depressing room. Unfortunately, she could only walk so slowly, so it wasn't long before she reached the fast-food restaurant on the corner across the street from the motel. She stopped to get herself some chicken nuggets and a salad, then she headed to the room she'd rented in the far corner of the motel, situated well away from the street.

Olivia slipped inside, locked the door, and, for good measure, propped the only chair in the room under the knob. Only then did she relax. As she took off her jacket, her fingers got tangled in the scarf her sister, Caitlin, had given her for Christmas almost four years ago.

"Open it." Caitlin giggled as she handed the gift to her sister, the smile on her face almost shy.

"I told you not to buy me anything," Olivia scolded.

"I didn't buy you anything," Caitlin said. "Now, open it."

Olivia tucked her feet beneath her and put the present on her lap. She smiled at the makeshift wrapping, almost as if a child had done it, even though Caitlin was seventeen. Caitlin wasn't good at wrapping gifts; she loved that about her sister. While Olivia and her mother fussed over every corner, every piece of tape and ribbon, Caitlin wrapped like she lived—without a care in the world.

Olivia unwrapped the gift, the brightly colored paper falling to the floor. She gasped as she pulled the thick, luxurious material free and spread it across her lap.

"It's beautiful." Tears pricked the corners of her eyes. It really was beautiful, soft and a lovely shade of royal blue that would bring out the blue in her eyes. She ran her hand back and forth over the decadent fabric, reveling in its beauty.

Caitlin picked it up and wrapped it around her sister's neck. "I made it, Liv."

Olivia laughed and swiped at the tears on her cheeks. "You did not."

"I did!" Caitlin insisted. "I crocheted it. It took me six months to get it right."

"It's gorgeous. You did an amazing job. I love it." Olivia hugged her. "And I love you too." She kissed Caitlin's cheek.

Caitlin smiled at her and blushed. "Love you too, sis."

A sharp knock jolted Olivia back to the present. "Ms. Miller?"

Olivia stepped close to the door and put her hand on the gun she kept on a nearby table. She rested her other hand on the motel door and took a deep breath to steady herself.

"Mr. Washburn? Is that you?" she called.

"It is," the man replied. "I was just checking on you."

"I'm good. Back safe from work."

"Everything all right?" the motel owner asked.

"Yes, sir." Olivia cleared her throat. "Thank you for checking on me."

"You're welcome," Mr. Washburn said. "Let me know if you need anything."

"I will," Olivia replied. "Thank you, again."

Chapter 1

Mr. Washburn mumbled something incoherent before Olivia heard him walk away. Every night, he stopped by her room to make sure she arrived safe and sound from the bank. At first it had annoyed her, even frightened her a little, but it wasn't long before she appreciated him taking the time to check on her.

Olivia carried her dinner to one of the two twin beds in the room and made herself comfortable. She only ate a few bites before she ended up pushing the food around in circles on her plate. Her stomach twisted in knots, so she dropped the salad on the bedside table and put her head in her hands.

She wished she wasn't here. She was sick of running, sick of hiding. If she could go back in time, she could fix this. Olivia wanted what they had taken from her. She wanted her life back.

Everything she had gone through weighed on her, making it hard to breathe. Her hands shook, and tears leaked from the corner of her eyes.

It's okay. I'm okay.

If she repeated it enough, maybe it would be true.

Olivia let the tears come and the emotions overwhelm her. If she bottled them up, kept them pushed down, they would tear her apart. In order to keep it from happening, every couple of weeks, she let herself go through all the emotions she tried to keep buried inside of her.

However, she refused to sit there, feeling sorry for herself. She swapped her clothes for a pair of yoga pants and an oversized t-shirt, then threw on a sweatshirt and her running shoes and opened the door. For the next forty-five minutes, she jogged around the empty parking lot, her head swiveling as she kept a watchful eye out for danger.

Once she had herself under control, she returned to her room, stripped off her clothes, folded them carefully, and put them in the shabby dresser. She put on a warm nightgown and wool socks, removed her colored contacts she wore to disguise herself, and washed her face. With her book in hand, she made herself comfortable on the bed. She threw a heavy quilt over her legs and opened her book. The picture fell out of the book and onto her lap.

Olivia stared at the photo for a long time after picking it up. It was a photo of her and her sister. She remembered the day they took the photo, less than two weeks after her father told her she was to be married. Caitlin had an arm thrown over her sister's shoulder and a wide smile on her face. She didn't know that Olivia would soon move out of their childhood home and into the home of one of their family's greatest enemies. Olivia had smiled for the camera, despite feeling like her father shattered her heart into pieces.

Olivia squeezed her eyes closed, trying to stop the memories that came so often and hurt so much. She kept the photo in her hand; it was the only one she had left. She'd deleted everything from her phone when she'd destroyed her SIM card.

She fell asleep with the book propped on her stomach and the picture between her fingers.

A week later, Olivia checked the clock, and, of course, it was fifteen minutes until closing. It drove her crazy that her eyes seemed drawn to that damn clock every day at a quarter to five, taunting her with the time left until the bank closed. She tucked her hair behind her ear, closed

Chapter 1

the drawer, and slid the money across the counter to the elderly gentleman patiently waiting. She gave him her best smile and thanked him, smiling even wider when he took his wife's arm and tucked her hand into the crook of his elbow as he led her out the door.

With a sigh, she glanced at the clock again. Thirteen more minutes until the bank closed and another night of misery began. Every day, she struggled to overcome the constant flood of negative emotions in her head. Olivia bit the inside of her cheek and reminded herself not to cry, not here, not in front of these people she didn't know.

The door opened, the bell over it chiming. Mr. Sewell stepped through the door, his entrance predictable, coming at the same time every day. A man in a suit and long coat with a fancy Fedora hat pulled down low over his eyes came in directly behind him. Olivia didn't think he was a regular customer; she had never seen him in the bank before. He stopped inside the door, as if he was waiting for something or someone.

Mr. Sewell gave her his usual friendly smile and hurried toward her, brown paper bag in hand, drawing her attention away from the man by the door.

"Good evening, Mr. Sewell," she smiled.

"Now, Ms. Miller, how many times have I asked you to call me Billy?" he teased.

"Almost every time I see you," she laughed. Mr. Sewell was fast becoming one of her favorite customers. He always had a smile and a kind word for her. "What can I do for you today?"

He'd just handed over his daily deposit when the double doors flew open and three men spilled into the bank, joining the man by the door. All of them wore

similar long coats and had their hats pulled low over their eyes. Three guns appeared, pointed at the ceiling.

"Hit the ground!" the man in the front yelled. "Heads down and hands flat on the floor." He waited for everyone to obey, then he strode purposefully toward Olivia.

Olivia stood dumbstruck, too scared to move. Her vision narrowed as the man walked toward her. She didn't see anything or anyone else, only him. He carried himself like a man who knew what he was doing; danger and menace rolling off him in waves. He pulled a gun from beneath his long coat and pointed it at her.

"Hands up. Do not even think about hitting that button," he said, mentioning the alarm under the counter. "Do you understand me?"

Olivia nodded.

"Good. Now, you're coming with me, sweetheart," he said. "I need you to open the vault."

Chapter 2
Declan

Declan called the shots; it didn't matter if the other men appreciated his methods. They didn't question him. Declan Quinn was in charge. Period.

Once everyone was on the bank floor, Declan gestured to the doors, the signal to barricade them. The men behind him turned, as if they were one unit, to do as ordered. Only then did Declan move across the floor, headed for the pretty brunette behind the counter.

"Everybody put your cell phones on the floor next to your head," he heard Conor yell. "Take them out nice and slow, no sudden moves. We don't need any dead heroes today."

After a year, they had this down to a precise science. His men knew exactly what to do.

Declan stared at the woman on the other side of the counter. She seemed familiar, as if he'd seen her somewhere before. He ignored the feeling; she was just another scared bank teller, not anyone he knew.

"Put your hands up. Do not even think about hitting that button," he said. "Do you understand me?"

The woman nodded.

"Good. Now, you're coming with me, sweetheart," he said. "I need you to open the vault."

The woman didn't move; she stood behind the counter staring at him. After a few seconds, she blinked, and her eyes focused on him. "Wh-what?" she mumbled.

Declan hated it when they froze; it made this so much harder.

He sighed. "Where's the bank manager?" he asked.

"G-gone home," the woman stammered. "I-I'm the only employee here."

"Can you open the vault?" he asked.

The woman gripped the edge of the counter so hard, her knuckles turned white. She nodded, but a strangled moan fell from her lips.

Declan leaned over the counter. "Can you open it?" he asked again, his tone menacing.

"Y-yes," she whispered.

Declan put a hand on the counter, and, in one simple move, he vaulted over it. He loved the old banks in these small towns for precisely this reason. They hadn't upgraded their security: they hadn't put in the bulletproof glass, the door buzzers, or the new cameras. It made them easy targets for robbing.

Once he stood beside the woman, he pointed down the back hall with the gun in his hand, indicating she should walk in front of him. Despite the fear he sensed coming off her, she stood tall as she walked to the back of the bank. Her hands shook as she unlocked the vault and pulled open the heavy door.

Declan glanced inside, then let out a sharp whistle. Murphy and Walsh appeared seconds later and grabbed the empty bags stashed along the inside wall of the vault.

Chapter 2

Without a word, they loaded the bags with cash, bonds, and whatever else they could pull from the safe.

Declan took the woman's arm and moved her, so she stood against the wall opposite the open bank vault. He stood beside her. She closed her eyes and clenched her hands together in front of her.

"Quinn?" the man inside the vault called out to Declan. "I need some help in here."

The girl's eyes shot open as soon as Murphy called his name, and she snuck a look at him out of the corner of her eye.

"You're … you're Declan Quinn? That guy who has been robbing all the banks?" she asked. Her voice shook as she spoke.

"Damn it," he muttered under his breath. He glared at her. "Don't move," he ordered.

She nodded. Obviously, he scared her; scratch that, he terrified her. Her breath tore in and out of her throat, shallow and uneven, and tremors of fear rolled through her as she sagged against the wall. She knew who he was, and it terrified her.

Declan stepped into the vault. "What?" he snapped.

"Do you want the safety deposit boxes cleared out?" Murphy asked.

"No, leave them." Declan checked his watch. "We've got three minutes. Move your asses."

Murphy and Walsh scooped up the bags laden with money. Declan waited until they headed for the front of the bank before he wrapped a hand around the woman's elbow and dragged her down the hall behind him. Conor had stayed at the front of the bank to tie and blindfold the bank's patrons. He had lined them up along one wall: seated on the floor, hands secured in front of them,

11

black bags over their heads. Declan walked past them and stopped in front of Conor.

"Watch her," he ordered.

He released the tight grip he had on the woman's arm and stalked across the bank. He grabbed Murphy by the shoulder and swung him around.

"You idiot," he snapped. "How many goddamn times do I have to tell you not to use names?" He punctuated each word with a finger to the chest of the smaller man standing in front of him.

"I ... I'm sorry, sir," Murphy whined. "It slipped out."

An irritated sound emanated from Declan's throat. He took off his hat and pushed a hand through his short, light brown hair and over the back of his neck.

"Put her in the car," he said to Conor, gesturing at the woman. "We're taking her with us."

"We can't," Conor said. "What if someone comes looking for her?"

"We have no choice," Declan yelled, turning on his friend. "It's a chance we'll have to take. She knows who I am and, thanks to Murphy, she knows my name. We can't leave her here to talk to the cops. She is going with us."

"This is a bad idea," Conor said. "A colossally bad idea."

"Why can't we kill her?" Walsh raised his gun and pointed it at the woman's head.

She flinched and choked back a sob. Declan scowled and pointed a finger at Walsh.

"Put that damn gun down. We cannot kill her. Not here, not now. There isn't time. Now put her in the goddamn car!"

Walsh lowered his weapon, took her by the arm, and dragged her out the door. He hustled her into the back seat of their black Denali. Declan waited until Murphy

Chapter 2

and Conor had exited the bank and loaded the money in the back of the SUV before he climbed into the front seat. Walsh and Murphy got in the back on either side of the woman, while Conor got behind the wheel. No one had noticed the bank being robbed, which was exactly how Declan wanted it. If they hadn't had to take the woman hostage, this would have been the perfect job.

Declan pulled a black sack from the glove compartment and tossed it over his shoulder. He nodded at Murphy, who yanked it over the woman's head.

"Enjoy the ride, honey," Declan muttered. He tapped the dashboard. "Let's go."

Declan shifted uneasily and adjusted his coat before he glanced over his shoulder at the woman in the backseat. Not only had Murphy put the black sack over the woman's head, but he'd also tied her hands in front of her. Of course, they were bound too tight. Declan could see the thick rope biting into her skin and marking her. He considered reaching back and loosening the bindings, but he stopped himself; showing weakness wasn't an option.

Declan glared at the man driving the Denali. Nothing pissed him off more than his men arguing with him, but it was worse when it was Conor. Conor Sullivan was Declan's best friend, and his opinion was the only one that mattered as much as Declan's.

Conor's insistence that they not take the woman with them should have been his first clue this was a shitty idea. But she'd heard his name and seen his face. Declan couldn't afford to have her talking to the Feds; it would ruin everything. The only rational decision was to take her.

He didn't want to kill her, but if he had to, he would. If it came down to her or his brother Drew, there was no question who he would choose.

Conor's expression was unreadable, though Declan was sure he knew what the man was thinking.

Declan sighed. "Just say it."

"What the hell are you doing, Deck?" Conor whispered, keeping his voice low. "Taking that girl was stupid."

"No shit," Declan muttered. "Like I said, we didn't have a choice. She saw my face and fucking Murph said my name. She would have talked to the Feds, and then this would be all over. Drew would be dead."

"What are you going to do?" Conor asked.

"I don't know," he muttered. "I don't know."

As soon as the Denali pulled to a stop in front of the small house at the end of the dirt road, Declan opened the door and jumped out. He stalked up the driveway, stopped in front of the enormous red barn that dominated the property, and took out his cell phone. It was the only place he got reception out there in the middle of nowhere. He hit a button, held the phone to his ear, and waited.

It rang three times before there was an answer, a quiet "yes." No other conversation was necessary. Declan said, "It's done," and disconnected the call. He shoved his phone in his pocket, scrubbed a hand over his face, and stared into the winter sun.

When is this going to end?

He glanced toward the house just as Walsh pulled the woman from the Denali. She hit her head on the

Chapter 2

roof, then stumbled forward and fell to one knee. Walsh yanked her upright and dragged her inside.

Declan growled. He hated Walsh. Despised him, but Clyde had insisted one of his men be a part of Declan's crew. He couldn't say no; it wasn't an option. But he could talk to Walsh about how he treated the girl. She was already terrified; roughing her up was unnecessary.

He checked his watch. They probably had an hour, maybe two, before Clyde and his goons arrived for their latest payment. Declan headed for the house; it was time to talk to his prisoner.

Chapter 3
Olivia

"We have to go now, Liv," Tommy said. "If we don't leave right now, I don't know when another opportunity will come up."

Olivia nodded. She dropped to her knees and grabbed the duffel bag she'd hidden under the bed. She threw on a sweatshirt and hurried to the door.

The hallway was empty; no surprise since it was Tommy who usually guarded her door. They hurried through the house, down the back stairs, and out the back door. They darted across the lawn and into the woods at the rear of the property.

It wasn't until they were under the cover of the trees that they slowed to a walk. Tommy took her hand and squeezed it.

"I told you I'd get you out of there," he said.

Guilt flooded her, but she kept her mouth shut. Olivia needed Tommy's help to get off the Muldoon property. It wasn't her fault he misinterpreted their friendship for something more. Once they were far enough away from the mess she was in, Olivia would explain her feelings—or lack of feelings—to Tommy. She prayed he would understand.

Chapter 3

The car turned a corner onto a bumpy road and jolted Olivia awake. They had crammed her in this car and stuck her in the backseat between two men who reeked of sweat, dirt, and whiskey. After they pulled the sack over her head, one man tied her hands in front of her, the thick rope biting into her skin. Tears rolled down her cheeks, soaking into the sack covering her face. She must have cried herself to sleep during the drive.

She fought hard to keep her freedom, but someone took it away from her. Again. Worse than that, the person who took it was a man she thought she'd never see again.

The car stopped, and the engine cut out. Someone grabbed her arm and dragged her roughly from the car, her head hitting the roof on the way out. Pain blurred her vision. Olivia stumbled forward and fell to one knee, dirt and rocks biting into her skin. A thick, muscled arm wrapped around her waist and pulled her to her feet.

They took her up a few stairs, over a wooden patio, and into a stuffy space filled with the odor of beer, whiskey, and cigarettes. The next thing she knew, they dropped her on what had to be a bed and yanked off the sack covering her head. Her long brown hair fell over her face. The man who'd held the gun to her head stood in front of her, staring at her for a long minute, something unreadable in his eyes. He mumbled something about Declan being an idiot and shook his head before he turned and left, slamming the door behind him. She heard the key turn in the lock, and then she was alone.

Olivia forced herself to breathe in and out, nice and slow. She took a moment to look around the room, grimacing at the filth covering everything. Dirt and dust bunnies had spread throughout the room. A faint beer-and-cigarette scent permeated the air as Olivia noticed the smudged window. A scratchy sheet and a thin wool blanket covered the bed. Aside from the bed, the only other furnishings in the room were a chair and a bedside table. The overhead light had three of its five bulbs either missing or burned out; it barely illuminated the room. The window was open two inches, a breeze made the curtains lift and flutter, bringing biting cold into the room.

Olivia shivered. A late afternoon chill had settled over everything, the cold seeping into every corner. Her coat was in the break room at the bank, along with the scarf Caitlin made her for Christmas. Her sister's face flashed in her head when she closed her eyes. She bit her lip and promised herself she wouldn't cry, despite the dire circumstances in which she found herself.

Thinking of something else, Olivia remembered again she knew exactly who the man was who had robbed the bank. His name was Declan "Deck" Quinn, and he was the most notorious bank robber in the eastern United States. He had made his way through the northeastern states for the last year, maybe longer, hitting more banks than even the FBI cared to admit. Olivia had heard the rumors about him, terrifying rumors. They accused him of murdering an employee over a dollar, kidnapping and killing bank tellers, and slaying ten officers in Philadelphia. Those were just a *few* of the things she'd heard about him.

While the world knew Declan Quinn's name, his actual identity was a closely guarded secret. There was no one alive, outside of the men who worked with him,

Chapter 3

who knew what he looked like. Except, of course, Olivia. She had seen his face and heard his name.

Not that Olivia needed to hear his name to know who he was. The minute he spoke to her and those piercing emerald green eyes looked at her, she'd known who it was. A woman never forgot her first love.

Despite her hands being tied, she tried to wipe her face. The rope bit into her skin, causing welts to rise to the surface. Blood pooled in several spots and soaked into the rope. She attempted to loosen the rope with her teeth, but she only made it tighter. Frustration and irritation built in her chest until a scream threatened to tear itself from her throat. She needed to stay calm and take stock of her situation, or she wouldn't get out of this alive.

On the other side of the door, loud voices could be heard arguing. She couldn't make out what they were saying or who was speaking. A door slammed, and the argument stopped. Or maybe it just moved to a different location. She strained to hear something, anything, that would let her know what the men in the other room had planned for her. Specifically, what Declan Quinn had planned for her.

"Where's the girl?" a deep, whiskey-thick, raspy voice asked that she could hear.

"Bedroom," was the reply.

Olivia listened to the footsteps approach the door, unconsciously moving backward across the bed until her back hit the wall. She drew her knees up, pulled her skirt down to cover her legs, and wrapped her bound hands around them. The door opened, and Declan stepped inside, closing it quietly behind himself.

He stood in front of her, handsomely dressed in white shirtsleeves, vest, and tie. The meticulous way he dressed

struck her as odd. Olivia stared up at him; he had to be well over six feet tall. She wasn't exactly short, topping out at 5'10", but this man made her feel small. His broad shoulders, muscular, toned body, and his strong jawline, coupled with his piercing green eyes, made for an intimidating presence. A far cry from the skinny kid she remembered years before.

He wore a holster with his gun tucked into it beneath his left arm. He didn't speak; instead, he concentrated on unbuttoning the cuffs of his shirt and neatly rolling them up, his eyes not meeting hers. When he finished, he bent over and withdrew a knife from a strap fastened around his ankle.

Olivia sat up straight, refusing to cower as he walked toward her. He spun the knife nonchalantly in his hand, took hold of the rope binding her wrists, and yanked her back across the bed until she sat in front of him. He lifted the knife and sliced the rope, letting it fall to the bed between her knees. Without saying a word, he turned around, grabbed the chair, turned it backward, and straddled it, quickly replacing the knife in its strap. They stared at each for several seconds before he spoke.

Does he remember me?

"What's your husband's name?" he asked quietly, pointing at the ring she wore on her finger.

Olivia flinched. She had never been married; she only wore the ring to keep would-be suitors at bay. "My husband is dead," she replied. She didn't offer any additional information.

Declan stared at her, which put her on edge. Was he staring at her because he remembered who she was, or was it because he was going to kill her? Maybe he was wondering how messy it would be if he sliced her open

Chapter 3

and let her bleed out on the floor. Instead, he sat calmly in front of her.

"You're a widow," he said. He scratched the side of his nose. "What about your parents?"

It was obvious Declan didn't remember her. Which meant there was no way she would tell him who her parents were. "My parents are dead," she lied.

"So, you're all alone," Declan said coldly.

A lump rose in her throat, and angry tears burned in the corner of her eyes. "Thank you for your sympathy," she snapped. This wasn't the Declan she had once loved; this Declan was a monster, a man who obviously understood nothing about pain and loss. "How many people have you murdered? How many wives and children have *you* left without a husband or a father? I've heard all the stories about you. All of them."

Olivia put her head in hands and dragged in a deep breath. Somehow, after everything she had gone through, she ended up with a man just like the one she had run away from. She rubbed her eyes and stared at the man across from her. Declan wasn't the person she remembered. No surprise: it had been eight years since they'd last seen each other.

Declan shook his head, his expression unreadable. His jaw twitched, and his lips tightened. She saw his throat move as he swallowed and took a deep breath.

The room was silent as they stared at each other: the only sound the mumbles of the men on the other side of the door, a car engine, and a slamming door on the other side of the house.

"What's your name?" Declan asked, breaking the silence.

For the first time in three years, she wanted to use her family name, scare him into releasing her. He would remember her then. Knowing her luck, it would backfire, and she'd get herself killed sooner rather than later. She had to be smart.

She cleared her throat. "Olivia Miller. And you're Declan Quinn." She tried to sound confident, but her voice wavered, and she couldn't look into his green eyes.

"You know who I am," he stated.

A sharp knock at the door drew his attention away from her. He rose slowly to his feet and yanked open the door. "What?"

"He's here," the stocky man at the door replied. "His car just turned into the drive."

"Shit." Declan's back straightened, and he squared his shoulders. He swung around and pointed a finger at Olivia. "If you want to stay alive, do not move and do not make a sound. For Christ's sake, do not even breathe loud." He disappeared through the door, slamming it behind him and throwing the lock, shouting orders at his men. A minute later, another door opened and closed, and an eerie silence settled over the house.

Chapter 4
Olivia

Olivia hesitated only a moment after Declan left the room before she rose to her feet. She rubbed her sore wrists as she crossed the room to pull back the flimsy, dust-covered curtain. She peered out, careful to stay out of sight of whoever was driving up. Declan sounded serious when he told her to stay quiet. She needed to know why.

Parked in the driveway was a large, red SUV. Two men in expensive suits stood beside it while another sat in the backseat with the door open. All she could see were his feet. Declan's men faced the car, their backs to the house. Declan joined them a few seconds later. Their quiet voices drifted through the air, but she couldn't hear them well. She carefully eased open the window a few inches, as she needed to hear what they said.

"Where's my brother?" Declan asked.

A short, balding man in a black suit stepped out of the SUV. Olivia gasped and stepped away from the window, shoving herself into the corner. She moaned and shook her head.

This can't be happening.

The man who had stepped out of the SUV was Clyde Braniff; Olivia knew him well. If he knew she was alive, if he knew she was here, he would mow down everyone in his path to possess her.

Fear twisted around her heart, and her blood ran cold. Declan scared her, but Clyde absolutely terrified her. If Declan told Clyde she was his prisoner, or God forbid, if Declan gave her to Clyde, death would be just around the corner.

Olivia bent over, put her hands on her knees, and dragged in several deep breaths. She had to calm down and could not freak out. Glancing around the room, she tried to find a way out while everyone was distracted. The door was locked, leaving the window as her only option. With no escape in sight, she was trapped. She pushed her fear aside and looked out the window again, careful to keep herself concealed behind the curtain. Fortunately, the approaching darkness would help hide her.

Please don't let him see me.

Clyde crossed his arms and looked Declan up and down. "I'm here for my money," he said. There was a faint Irish lilt in his voice that Olivia remembered well. It sent a chill down her spine to hear it.

Declan nodded to the man beside him, one of the men Olivia saw at the bank, who separated from the group and walked back to the house. Olivia lost sight of him for a minute, but then he reappeared with two bank bags in his hands. He handed them to one of Clyde's men, who put them in the back of the SUV.

Clyde crossed his arms over his chest. "I understand that you have a visitor. A girl?"

Declan scrubbed the back of his neck and shook his head. "No, no visitors. One of the bank employees

Chapter 4

saw my face and heard my name. But there's nothing to worry about. I took care of it. I killed her and dumped the body," he said.

"You didn't keep her?" Clyde asked. He looked at the other men standing with Declan. "She might have been good ... entertainment." He chuckled, a dry, evil sound.

"I don't need some bitch hanging around causing problems."

Clyde nodded, apparently satisfied with Declan's answer. When Declan looked away, Clyde glanced at one of his men and then at the house, a subtle tilt of his head no one else noticed, except for Olivia. She dropped the curtain and stepped away from the window.

Why did Declan lie to Clyde?

Olivia waited, counting to thirty in her head before she looked out the window again. As she watched, Clyde turned to the SUV and gestured to someone inside. A lanky, young man with shaggy brown hair unfolded himself from the back seat and stepped out of the car. At his full height, he stood several inches above Declan. One of Clyde's men pulled a gun from inside his jacket and held it at his side.

"Hey, Deck," the young man said. His voice cracked on the last word, and Olivia thought he might be close to crying.

"Drew," Declan said. He took one step forward, but the man with the gun pointed the weapon at him.

"You know the rules, Quinn," Clyde snapped. "Money for proof of life. A deal is a deal. Say hello but stay put."

Declan growled, his shoulders tense and his fists clenched. "It's been more than a year, Clyde—." One of Declan's men standing next to him put a hand on his arm and squeezed tightly.

"I know how long it's been," Clyde said.

"You said one year," Declan said. "One year if I did as you asked. And I have done as you asked repeatedly, even after what you did to Sarah." He let out a long, shuddering breath. "Just let my brother go, and we'll be on our way. You have more than enough money."

Clyde threw his head back and laughed, the harsh sound echoing through the night. "Oh, Deck, it will never be enough. There is no such thing as 'enough money.' If you want your brother to live, you keep doing what I want. You have no choice." He turned to the younger man. "Get back in the car."

The young man—Drew—nodded and climbed back into the SUV. He hunched over and put his head in his hands.

Declan took another step toward the SUV, but the man beside him grabbed his arm and held him back. He whispered something in Declan's ear, something that made Declan drop his head and step back.

Clyde laughed. "Good boy. You do as you're told." He got in beside Drew and slammed the car door.

Declan stood in the driveway until the SUV was out of sight and the dust settled. It wasn't until it was out of sight that he turned back and returned to the house.

Olivia carefully shut the window and returned to her seat on the bed. She tried to process everything she had just seen and heard, tried to make sense of it.

Apparently, Declan worked for Clyde, a man she hated and feared. If Declan found out who she was, if he *remembered* who she was, he wouldn't hesitate to turn her over to the mobster. Clyde would be more than happy to hand over Declan's brother for her.

Chapter 4

She was a bargaining chip. An extremely important bargaining chip that Declan didn't know he possessed. She meant to keep it that way.

The exchange between Declan and Clyde brought up more questions than answers for Olivia. Unfortunately, she couldn't ask the questions she desperately wanted answered because it would give her identity away. She would have to keep quiet and play dumb to survive.

Olivia sat on the bed and watched the door, expecting Declan to walk through it at any minute. It wouldn't surprise her if he came to end her life, to do what he told Clyde he'd already done. A strange sense of calm came over her at the thought that all of this would be over soon. At least she wouldn't have to run anymore.

According to the watch on her wrist it was almost midnight; three hours had passed before she heard the key turning in the lock. Declan entered with a sandwich and a glass of water, which he put on the bedside table without a word. He was almost outside the door when she spoke.

"Why did you lie?" she asked. "To that man, about me?"

Declan froze and turned around. "You heard?" He glared at her, his jaw clenched, his hands in fists at his side. Anger rolled off him in thick, heated waves. "How much did you hear?"

Olivia shrugged. "Not much." She stared at her hands, unable to meet his eyes. "But I heard you say you killed me. Why did you lie?"

He was quiet for a few seconds before he answered. "I don't know."

Olivia swallowed around the lump in her throat. "What are you going to do with me?" she asked.

Declan sighed. "I'm not sure yet." His dress shirt tightened across his muscular shoulders and chest as he took a deep breath. He shook his head, as if he was having some internal argument with himself. He didn't say anything else; instead, he flung open the door and left, leaving her alone with her thoughts.

Olivia took a deep breath. She couldn't wait any longer, and it was obvious no one was going to step up and offer to help her. She pounded on the door.

"Hello?" she yelled.

Loud footsteps crossed the hardwood floor, then they inserted a key into the lock. She took a step back and pushed a hand through her hair. She wondered who would open the door.

It wasn't who she expected. The man who opened the door was shorter than Declan, though no less attractive: his red hair was short; he was clean-shaven; and his eyes were hazel. He had on jeans and a black-and-green flannel shirt. She recognized him from the bank; he had stayed in the lobby while Declan and his men had taken her back to the vault.

"Did you need something?" he asked, concerned.

"A bathroom," she croaked. "Please?"

The man nodded. He stepped in, took hold of her elbow, and led her out of the bedroom. They crossed a small living room with a connected kitchen. He took her down a short hallway and stopped in front of an open door. He gestured for her to go in.

Olivia went in, shut the door, and flipped the lock. She hurried to the toilet, breathing a sigh of relief when

Chapter 4

she could finally relieve herself. When she was done, she washed her hands and splashed some water on her face. Then she took the colored contacts out of her eyes and washed them down the drain. She left the water running while she looked around the room. There was a tiny window, maybe two feet by two feet, and covered in thick, opaque glass. There was nothing on the sink or near the bathtub she could use as a weapon, so she checked the drawers and medicine cabinet, hoping to find something she could use.

Unfortunately, the drawers only held cotton balls, nearly empty toothpaste tubes, deodorant, and two bottles of aspirin. The medicine cabinet was empty. Under the sink, she found three rolls of toilet paper and a stack of towels.

A knock on the door made her jump. She twisted off the water and opened the door.

"Are you done?" the man asked impatiently.

Olivia nodded. He took her arm again and led her back to the bedroom. It wasn't until they were crossing the living room that she realized no one else was in the house; it was just her and this man. She wondered where the others were. She stepped into the bedroom and turned to look at him.

"Thank you, um—."

"Conor," he responded. "My name is Conor."

Conor Sullivan, Declan's best friend. Olivia remembered Conor helping her and Declan sneak off to see each other after her father had forbidden their relationship. He must not remember her either.

"Thank you, Conor," she mumbled.

He gave her an odd look, almost as if he was trying to remember something, or had noticed something about her. After a few seconds, he gave her a curt nod and pulled the door closed.

Chapter 5
Olivia

The sun streaming through the thin curtains woke Olivia the next morning. She stretched, one hand hitting the wall above her head. She rolled to her side, wrapped her arms around her legs, and tried not to shiver. The thin blanket covering her wasn't enough to keep her warm. She concentrated on breathing in through her nose and out through her mouth, hoping to take her mind off the bitter cold seeping into her bones.

For a moment, she forgot where she was, and that she was a prisoner, the captive of a man who would probably kill her. The emptiness beside her brought reality rushing back into her mind, reminding her she was alone, cold, and trapped in a small, locked room. Fear clutched at her heart.

She ignored the sharp knock at the door soon after waking. Whoever it was could go away and leave her alone. But the knock came again.

"Go away!" she yelled. She squeezed her eyes shut and hugged her legs tight against her body. She wanted to be left alone.

Instead, the door swung open on creaky hinges. She opened her eyes and saw Declan's broad shoulders filling the doorframe.

Olivia sighed; a bone-deep shudder worked its way through her, and her teeth chattered. Declan grumbled something incoherent and disappeared, leaving the door wide open. She smelled cigarette smoke and heard men talking. She opened her eyes and saw two men sitting at a small table covered in bowls and coffee mugs. A television played behind them and, just a few feet past them, was another door. The door that led outside, that led to freedom.

Declan reappeared with a heavy quilt clutched in his hands. He stalked across the room, unfolding it as he approached. He stopped at the side of the bed, shook it out, and let it fall on her. It covered her from head to toe. The door closed a few seconds later, the lock clicking into place.

She burrowed beneath the quilt, pulling it over her head, letting its warmth surround her. Maybe the Declan she had known all those years ago was still in there somewhere. If he planned on killing her, why give her a quilt to keep her warm? It didn't make sense.

For the thousandth time in the last twelve hours, she wondered if she should tell Declan who she was. If he knew she was Liv O'Reilly, not Olivia Miller, he might let her go. Then again, he might turn her over to Clyde.

She hadn't felt so helpless since her father sent her to live with the Muldoons, her future in-laws. It was supposed to help ease her mind, allow her to get to know her future family before the wedding took place. However, Sean O'Reilly didn't know the horrible position he put his daughter in.

Chapter 5

Even though Olivia was supposedly free to come and go as she pleased from the Muldoon compound, she was a prisoner, and she knew it. Everywhere she went, a bodyguard accompanied her. She was worth too much; half of her four-million-dollar dowry sat in an offshore account, and her father held the other half. Her future uncle-in-law, Donovan Muldoon would receive the money once she said the vows.

Her life in exchange for four million dollars and the promise of peace between the Muldoons and the O'Reillys, two big mob families. According to her father, it was a small sacrifice.

The male heir to the Muldoon empire was her betrothed, Clyde Braniff, who was also Donovan Muldoon's nephew. Donovan Muldoon never had children of his own, forcing him to leave his fortune and the family business to his sister's son. Clyde terrified her. He was the cruelest man she'd ever met. A psychopath without empathy for others, a man who cared only about himself and the power he could attain. He viewed Olivia as property and nothing more.

Things hadn't been so bad at first; Clyde was out of the country on an extended home visit to Ireland, so her first two months at the compound were without his presence. She was taken aback by the kindness Donovan Muldoon showed her. He gave her a suite of rooms on the west end of the mansion and left her alone. She could leave the compound to eat, go shopping, and, of course, plan her wedding, as long as her bodyguard was with her.

Her bodyguard was Tommy Byrne, the man she sometimes said was her husband. They became friends, inevitable when two people spent as much time together as they did. It wasn't long before Tommy declared his love for her.

Olivia never encouraged Tommy's feelings, but she didn't discourage them either. She realized having Tommy on her side would be beneficial but never realized just how much. So, she flirted with him and played up the unhappy woman bit. It was a shame she didn't understand how close to the truth it was until it was too late.

It wasn't until Clyde came back from his visit to Ireland that Olivia realized how desperate her situation had become. Clyde wasn't back for a full week before he hit her the first time. She spilled a glass of red wine on the dining room table, staining the white tablecloth. Olivia apologized, noting that Donovan didn't care about one ruined tablecloth. Once they left the dining room, Clyde backhanded her and scolded her like a child.

It came as a shock. She was the daughter of an O'Reilly; no one had ever dared to lay a finger on her. Her father would kill any man who hurt her. Things only got worse; to Clyde, Olivia wasn't human. She was his property to do with as he pleased. And that was exactly what he did.

After he raped her the first time, he beat her bloody and left her on the floor of her bathroom. He didn't stop there; he came to her room three or four times a week and forced himself on her every time. The sick bastard liked it when she fought back. Clyde took from her whenever and however he wanted.

However, Olivia refused to let him break her.

Clyde took her phone, isolating her and making it impossible for her to contact her family. He kept her locked in her room for extended periods of time, lying to Donovan about where she was and what she was doing. The bruises and marks got harder to hide until even

Chapter 5

Donovan Muldoon noticed them. After a while, Tommy noticed them and did something about it.

The door swung open, interrupting her thoughts. The big ugly guy, the one who threw her in this room, stepped inside, dropped a plate of food on the table, then turned and left, slamming the door closed behind him.

Olivia threw off the quilt and climbed out of the bed. The sandwich looked edible, and the carrot sticks seemed fresh, so she sat in the chair at the table and picked at the food. What she wouldn't give for a cup of coffee.

She glanced at the door. Last time she was a prisoner, Tommy had swooped in and rescued her, taking her away from the pain and heartbreak. This time, Olivia would have to rescue herself.

Tired of sitting in one spot, Olivia crossed to the window and pulled the curtain aside. The world outside was an odd orangish-brown color, thanks to the setting sun and overcast sky. There was nothing around for miles, no other buildings aside from the house and a large, red barn. There was only one road leading to the house and fields as far as she could see. Not only was it overcast, but it was cold as well. She could feel the chill seeping through the shoddily built walls and the poorly sealed window.

It had been a little over twenty-four hours since Declan took her from the bank. She didn't know what he wanted or what his intentions were. All she knew was she had to figure out a way out of this place. Olivia couldn't wait around to see what he would do, whether he would give her to Clyde or choose to kill her. Not that it mattered; either way, she was dead.

A dark-colored SUV turned onto the dirt road leading to the house. Olivia watched as it approached and came to a stop in front of the house. Declan climbed out of the driver's side, while the other two men climbed out of the back seat. They went around to the back, unloaded several bags, and carried them into the house. Their voices filled the front room.

Olivia went back to the bed and sat down. She stared at the wall, counting the small, pink flowers on the shabby wallpaper and letting her mind drift.

It wasn't easy to stay in the booth, not when Declan was only a few feet away. She missed him so much it hurt. She crossed her fingers and squeezed her eyes shut, praying Declan would do the right thing.

"You need to stay away from Liv, Mr. Quinn," Grady McCarthy, her father's second-in-command, said.

"I can't do that. I love her," Declan replied.

Olivia's heart skipped a beat. He loved her.

Grady snorted. "That doesn't matter. You need to stay away from here. Her father's orders."

"What if I don't?" Declan asked.

Grady's voice dropped an octave. "You will regret it." There was a pause, then Grady continued. "Look, Declan, don't make this harder than it has to be. You work for the Muldoons. Did you really think Sean O'Reilly would let you ride off into the sunset with his daughter? Walk away now, and nothing will happen. Liv will find someone else and you, well, Declan, you will get to live. Understood?"

Grady pushed himself out of the booth. Olivia ducked her head, but before she knew what was happening, Grady

Chapter 5

took her arm, dragged her out of her seat, and pushed her through the restaurant in front of him. She glimpsed Declan sitting in their booth, an angry scowl marring his handsome face.

"Forget about him, Liv," Grady said. "Or he's history."

Olivia sighed and put her head in her hands. Even if Declan remembered her, did he remember the words he said that day? Did he remember he said he loved her? Because she had never forgotten.

She got to her feet and paced the room. Declan wasn't the same man she had loved when she was nineteen years old. He was cold, impersonal, frightening. He worked for Clyde Braniff and if he knew who she was, he would turn her over to him. She couldn't let him know. Any feelings she might still have for him had to be pushed down deep and ignored. It was the only way she could stay safe.

Chapter 6
Declan

Olivia was on her feet when he opened the door. She crossed her arms over her chest and stared at him.

"What are you going to do with me?" she asked. Or maybe demanded was a better way of putting it. She was on fire, ready to do battle. He wasn't in the mood to deal with a fired-up, angry woman today. Especially since he still wasn't sure what he was going to do with her.

Declan held his tongue, sighed, and set the tray of food on the bedside table. "I told you; I don't know." He took a step back and crossed his arms over his chest. "Any other questions?"

Olivia shook her head and took a deep breath before she spoke. "If you let me go, I swear I won't tell anyone who you are. I won't tell them what you look like or who is with you. I won't even tell them about Clyde."

Declan narrowed his eyes and took a step closer to her. "What did you say?"

Realization dawned in Olivia's eyes. She put her hands over her mouth and took a step back.

He had never mentioned Clyde's name to Olivia; none of them had. But somehow, she knew who he was.

"How do you know Clyde Braniff?" he asked.

Chapter 6

Olivia dropped her hands from her mouth and clenched them in front of her, twisting them together. "I don't," she whispered.

"You're lying," Declan snapped.

Olivia swallowed, opened her mouth, and closed it again. She shook her head.

Declan crossed the room in two quick strides, grabbed Olivia by her shoulders, and shoved her against the wall. He held her there with one hand on her throat and the other braced on the wall by her head. He leaned over her.

"How the hell do you know Clyde Braniff?" he repeated.

Olivia gasped, her eyes going to the window, the floor, then back to him. "Let me go."

"Answer the question, Olivia. Tell me how you know Clyde."

Olivia's tongue darted out, wetting her lips. She closed her eyes. "I'm ... uh, I'm from the Boston area. You can't live there and *not* know the Muldoons." She shifted uneasily. "Or the O'Reilly family."

Declan leaned over her. A low growl came from his throat. "Who are you?" he asked.

"Nobody," Olivia mumbled. "I'm just a nobody."

"I don't believe you." He released her, spun around, and walked back to yank open the door. He turned back to look at her.

"You're lying. I don't know why, but you are." He slammed the door and locked it.

Walsh was in his face as soon as he turned back around. His voice was low, quiet, and angry. "What the hell was that, Deck?"

Declan glared at him. "What are you talking about?"

"What is she lying about?" Walsh asked. "And why do we care?"

"It's not important," Declan muttered.

"It sounds like it is," Walsh said. "Maybe you should stop treating her like you're going to let her live."

"What makes you think I'm not going to kill her?" Declan took a step toward Walsh, who wisely backed up.

"You have no choice," Walsh said. He pointed at the door, punctuating each word with a jab of his finger toward the bedroom. "That woman has seen our faces; she knows our names, and she is in our safe house, which means it is no longer safe. Clyde already thinks she is dead. What happens when he finds out you let a witness live?"

Declan lunged at Walsh, grabbed the front of his shirt, and jerked him close, bringing them nose to nose. "How would he find out?"

Walsh shrugged, a smile playing at the corner of his mouth. "Someone might tell him. You never know."

Declan shoved Walsh into the wall next to the door, his arm poised to hit the smug bastard in the face, but before he could, Conor pushed himself between them and put his hand on Declan's chest.

"Talk a walk, Walsh," Conor ordered, pointing at the front door. "Go cool off somewhere else before I let Declan kick your ass."

Walsh snorted, but he did as he was told. He grabbed his jacket and stomped out the door. Conor looked at Murphy and tipped his head. Murphy got up without a word and took his coffee to the back of the house.

Conor turned on his best friend. "What the fuck, Declan?"

Declan shook a cigarette out of the package in his pocket and lit it. He took a deep drag and stared at the floor. He shook his head. "I don't know. Walsh sets me off."

Chapter 6

Conor sat on the edge of the recliner. "He has always set you off. If I hadn't stepped between you two, you would have taken him out."

Declan shrugged, a frown on his face. "If he tells Clyde she's alive—."

"He won't," Conor interjected. "I'll make sure of it."

Declan nodded. "Just keep an eye on him. Make sure he doesn't contact Clyde. Also, I need you to do something for me."

Conor snorted. "You mean something else?"

"Yeah. I need you to put your computer and research skills to the test and find out who Olivia really is."

"What do you mean?" Conor asked. "I don't understand."

"I don't think Olivia Miller is who she says she is," Declan explained. "She's not just a widow living in a tiny Pennsylvania town working at a bank. She slipped up. When I was in there talking to her, she told me she wouldn't tell the Feds about Clyde. Even though none of us ever mentioned his name to her, she still knows it. She mentioned the Muldoons and the O'Reillys too. She said it was because she's from Boston, but I don't believe her. I want answers. I need you to dig, find out everything you can about her."

Conor pushed himself out of the chair. "On it, boss."

Declan crossed his arms over his chest and tried to get comfortable in the small recliner. His feet hung off the end, and a loose coil poked him in the back. He could have slept in the master bedroom on the cot they'd set up, but he'd taken the first watch and then the second watch when he couldn't sleep. Walsh hadn't complained; he willingly went back to bed.

Declan had slept little the last year. Most nights he'd get two or three hours or, if he was lucky, four. Ever since Clyde took Sarah from him and kidnapped Drew, sleep had been an elusive friend he couldn't quite capture.

For the last year, three months, and twenty-four days, Clyde had controlled his life, using his brother to keep him in line. Declan couldn't escape, not as long as Clyde had Drew. He had to do what Clyde wanted. He had no choice.

Declan must have dozed off because the next time he opened his eyes, the light had changed. He groaned and sat up.

"Morning, sunshine," Conor said. He tapped the ashes from the tip of his cigarette into a ceramic bowl on the table.

"What time is it?" Declan asked.

Conor checked his watch. "A few minutes after six. Walsh and Murphy are still asleep." He shifted in his seat and pointed at the laptop on the table. "I need to show you something."

"Is there coffee?"

Conor nodded. "Yeah." He pointed at the pot on the table. "It's fresh. I just made it."

Declan climbed out of the chair, groaning as his back spasmed and his neck popped. He grabbed a Mickey Mouse mug off the counter, returned to the table, and dropped into the chair beside Conor. He filled the mug with coffee, took a sip, and looked at his best friend.

"I take it you found something?" Declan asked.

"Oh yeah, I definitely found something." He put the computer in front of Declan and tapped the screen.

Chapter 6

On it was a picture of Clyde with a woman. They must have taken it when they were on the move because it was blurry and out of focus. Declan couldn't see much of the woman, just a vague profile and dark blonde hair.

"What am I looking at?"

Conor tapped the computer screen. "I think that's Olivia," he said.

Declan sat up straight. "What? You think that's Olivia *with* Clyde?"

Conor took another drag of his cigarette. "Yeah, I do." He tapped more ashes into the ceramic dish. "Do you know how many Olivia Millers there are in the United States?"

"I'm guessing a lot," Declan replied.

"Yeah, a lot. But not one of them lives in Pennsylvania and works at a bank." Conor tapped the keyboard on the laptop and opened another screen. "It took some digging, but I found an Olivia Miller staying at a cheap motel a few blocks from the bank. She's only been there for a couple of months, and she always pays for her room in cash. I pulled the employee records from the bank. Olivia has worked there for six weeks. Prior to that, I can't find anything about an Olivia Miller in northern Pennsylvania."

"So, you hit a dead end?"

Conor shook his head. "I thought I did, so I switched to Clyde. And found that photo." He switched the screen back to the photo of Clyde and the blurry, out-of-focus female. "I thought the woman in the photo looked familiar. But you know how it is. People you've never seen before look familiar because they look like somebody you *do* know. I convinced myself I was wrong, that she wasn't who I thought she was."

"Conor," Declan said. "Get to the point."

"I'm getting there. Be patient." Conor cleared his throat. "Do you remember Liv O'Reilly?"

Declan nodded. "That's a stupid question. Of course, I remember Liv. Sean O'Reilly's daughter. I was head over heels in love with her. I wanted to fucking marry her until her father stepped in and forced us to end the relationship. He decided I was a bad influence. It didn't help that we ran with the Muldoons. I haven't seen her in eight years, since she was nineteen and I was twenty-two."

"Did you know she was supposed to marry Clyde?"

Declan gritted his teeth and snarled. "Yeah. Her marriage to Clyde was supposed to unite the two families and end the tension in Boston's South End. But it didn't happen."

"Rumor has it one of Clyde's men, Tommy Byrne, got her out," Conor said. "He did it because he was in love with her. He got her out, and then she dumped him. She supposedly took two million dollars, money Sean O'Reilly earmarked as a payoff to Donovan Muldoon, a dowry of sorts; that was three years ago."

Declan squinted at the screen. "I thought they found her and Tommy?"

Conor shook his head. "They found Tommy. Three months after they vanished, Tommy showed up at Finnegan's Bar and demanded a meeting with Sean O'Reilly. He was going to tell O'Reilly where his daughter was in exchange for O'Reilly's protection. O'Reilly agreed and hid Tommy in a shitty motel while they negotiated the terms of the agreement. Except Clyde's men found him first and killed him. Liv ghosted and has been MIA ever since. Not only is Clyde looking for her, but so is her father. He wants his daughter brought home in one piece; Clyde does not."

Chapter 6

"And you think we somehow stumbled on Liv O'Reilly in a tiny shithole town in northern Pennsylvania? Of all the people in the world for us to find, you think we found a mobster's missing daughter?"

"Yeah, I do," Conor said. "After we talked last night, my brain wouldn't shut down. I was trying to put the pieces together. I kept thinking she looked familiar, that somehow I knew something about her. Then I found that photo, and something clicked." He pointed at the bedroom door. "I remember Liv. How could I not? That woman in there looks like Liv, sounds like Liv, and she's the right age."

"It could be a coincidence," Declan suggested. "The Liv I remember was blonde and had blue eyes. Freckles. Not dark hair and green eyes."

Conor nodded. "I know. I thought the same thing. It's easy enough to dye hair and cover freckles with makeup. And she doesn't have green eyes anymore, Deck."

"What?"

"I took her to the bathroom the other night when you and the guys were dumping the cars. When she came out, her eyes were blue. I think she had colored contacts on. She must have dumped them down the drain." Conor sat forward. "Her eyes are blue now."

Declan jumped out of the chair and started pacing, walking back and forth across the small living room. "Even if she is Liv O'Reilly, we can't turn her over to Clyde. He'll kill her. And if we turn her over to her father, Clyde will see it as a betrayal and kill us. Maybe we should just let it go. Especially since we don't know for sure."

"That's just it, Deck. I know for sure."

Declan stopped pacing. "What?"

"I knew I needed to find a picture of Liv O'Reilly. Not the nineteen-year-old we hung out with when we were younger, but grown-up Liv. And not some crappy, out-of-focus picture that didn't answer our questions. So, I dug deeper. O'Reilly tried to keep her out of the spotlight, probably for her own safety, but he wasn't always successful." He tapped the computer screen again. "I kept looking and eventually, I found this."

Conor switched to another tab on the computer and swung it around to face Declan. On the screen was a photo of a younger Olivia Miller. She wore a gown made of a silver-and-black shiny fabric, and her dark blonde hair cascaded down her back in soft waves. She looked over her shoulder and winked at the camera.

Declan crossed the room until he could read the caption under the photo.

Liv O'Reilly, 24, daughter of Sean O'Reilly, local Boston real estate magnate, attends a gala at the Boston Museum of Fine Arts.

Conor sat back and crossed his arms over his chest, a smug smirk on his face.

"It's her. Olivia Miller is Liv O'Reilly."

Chapter 7
Olivia

It had been four days since Declan had taken Olivia from the bank and locked her in the tiny room. During that time, she had walked it repeatedly. Fifteen paces long and ten paces wide, a constant reminder of how cramped and unbearable it was.

The only person she had seen for the last four days was Declan. Every morning and every evening, he would unlock the door, set her food on the bedside table, and then he would escort her to the bathroom. Then he would walk her back to the bedroom and lock her in.

She hadn't asked him again about letting her go. After her last misstep, when she'd mentioned Clyde, she was too scared to speak. To her surprise, Declan hadn't mentioned it. She'd been sure he would push her for more information, especially after he accused her of lying. But he'd been silent, though now and then, she caught him giving her an odd look.

Maybe he believed she only knew Clyde because she was a Boston resident. He hadn't pushed her for answers or questioned her again. She was unsure whether to feel relieved or scared.

Olivia sat on the bed, wrapped in the heavy quilt Declan had given her, shivering; it was like being trapped in one of those huge walk-in refrigerators. Every inch of her ached from the cold permeating her bones. She glanced at the door, wondering if it was this cold in other parts of the house.

She pushed a hand through her hair, cringing as the greasy, dirty locks slid between her fingers. It had been days since she'd bathed; dirt and grime coated her. She tugged at the collar of the dress she had worn for almost four days and for the first time in three years, she wished she could go home.

Not home, as in the one-star motel she'd been hiding in, but *home*. Her parents' home. She missed her mother, her father, and her younger sister, Caitlin. Her father could have made all of this go away with a snap of his fingers. But she couldn't go home; not now, maybe never.

Hell, she'd be thrilled to be back at the shitty, one-star motel. Any place was better than this cramped, locked room with a brooding bank robber for company. One who still hadn't decided if she was going to live or die.

Olivia glanced at her watch. It was almost seven in the morning. Declan would be in soon if he stuck to the same schedule. Sure enough, ten minutes later, there was a movement on the other side of the door. Maybe today would be the day she would find out what her future held.

Promptly at seven-thirty, the door swung open. But instead of coming into the room with a sandwich and a glass of water, Declan stopped at the threshold, empty-handed. Olivia watched him warily.

"I made coffee," he said, then he walked away, leaving the door wide open.

Chapter 7

Olivia didn't move. Was this some kind of test? Or maybe a trick? She waited a full minute before she stood up, dropped the quilt on the bed, and moved to the doorway. She peered out, curious yet fearful of what Declan had planned. He stood at the counter pouring coffee into a Mickey Mouse coffee mug. She could see the gun tucked in the waistband of his jeans, but she could also see the steam wafting from the mug in front of him. The thick, rich scent of coffee made her mouth water.

Declan glanced at her out of the corner of his eye, grabbed a second mug, and filled it with coffee. He carried both mugs to the table, removed a stack of papers and a full ashtray, and put them on the table. Without uttering a single word, he pulled out a chair, took a seat, and began flipping through a magazine on the table. He acted as if pouring a cup of coffee for the woman he had been holding as a hostage for days was a common occurrence.

Olivia was unsure of Declan's ulterior motives—if he even had any—but the thought of a warm mug in her hands propelled her across the room. She sat gingerly in the chair across from Declan, picked up the steaming mug, and took a small sip. Warmth flooded her. She closed her eyes and sighed.

It was quiet, the only sound Declan turning the magazine pages. Absorbed in the wondrous taste and smell of the fresh coffee in her hands, it took Olivia a minute to realize it was *too* quiet. She looked around, but aside from her and Declan, the house appeared to be deserted. Olivia cleared her throat, drawing Declan's attention.

"Where is everyone?" she asked.

"I sent them to town for supplies," he replied. "They'll be back in a couple of hours."

Olivia cleared her throat. "You, uh, you didn't want to go with them?"

Declan stared at her. "Someone had to stay behind." He sipped his coffee nonchalantly. "I thought you might want to get out of the room for a while and get cleaned up. It's best if you don't have to deal with my men. They can be abrasive."

"Or you thought I'd try to escape," she muttered.

Declan chuckled. "I'm not worried about that. There is nowhere for you to go." He went back to reading the magazine.

"I want to go home," she blurted out.

Declan shrugged. "I'm sure you do," he said calmly. He didn't even bother to look at her.

Olivia sighed. "I don't understand. How long are you planning on keeping me here?"

Declan put the magazine on the table, sat back, and crossed his arms over his chest. "I don't know."

She slammed her hand down on the table. "That's not good enough. *I* need to know. You can't keep stringing me along." She shoved her chair away from the table and stumbled to her feet, sudden panic forcing her to move. She darted for the door, determined to run, even if there was nowhere for her to go.

Declan shot to his feet and grabbed her arm before she reached the door. He held her upper arms as he pushed her against the wall, his face just inches from hers.

"There is nowhere for you to go," he snapped.

Fear clutched her heart and squeezed. Tears leaked from the corner of her eyes. "Please, let me go. Like I told you, I won't tell anyone about you. I'll go away, and no one will find me."

"Clyde will find you," Declan said.

Chapter 7

"It's been three years, and Clyde Braniff hasn't found me yet!" she yelled. Her mouth snapped shut when she realized what she said.

"Oh, that's right, *Liv*," Declan said sarcastically, releasing her and stepping back. "You've been hiding from your former fiancé for what? Three years? You've gotten pretty good at it, haven't you?"

The air rushed out of Olivia's lungs as her head spun. She sagged against the wall and rubbed her arm where Declan had grabbed her. "You know who I am," she whispered.

"Yes, I know who you are." Declan scrubbed a hand over the back of his neck. "Liv O'Reilly. I figured it out two days ago."

"Do you ... do you remember me?" she asked. "Do you remember how close we were?"

Declan nodded, and his face softened. "Of course, I remember. How could I forget you? You were my entire world. I loved you."

"Don't say that," Olivia whispered.

"Why not? It's true. I would have gone to the ends of the earth for you. I wanted to spend the rest of my life with you," Declan said.

"My father never would have let it happen," Olivia said. "He thought you were a bad influence, and you ran with the Muldoons."

"But it was okay for him to marry you off to one of them?" Declan muttered.

Olivia laughed, the sound hollow and fake in her ears. The irony wasn't lost on her. None of it. "I never wanted that. Never."

Declan snorted. "So what? You were following instructions?"

Olivia wasn't going to explain her life and her pain to a man she hadn't seen for eight years, a man who had kidnapped her and was holding her hostage. "So, now what happens? You hand me over to Clyde? Maybe he'll give you your brother back for me."

"Don't think I haven't thought about it," Declan snapped.

Olivia's pulse raced, the desire to run so strong the muscles in her thighs twitched. "Is that what you're waiting for? The chance to hand me over to Clyde?"

Declan shook his head and sighed. "I know what happens if I give you to Clyde. I know what kind of person he is."

Olivia muttered, "I don't think you know everything."

Declan rose to his full height in confidence. "I know exactly what Clyde Braniff does to people who wrong him. You were supposed to marry him. But you embarrassed him by disappearing with one of your bodyguards and stealing his money. If Clyde gets his hands on you, it will not go well for you."

Declan moved closer, hovering over her where she leaned against the wall, a menacing, evil look on his face, his voice thick with emotion. "He will rape you, torture you, humiliate you, and degrade you. He will do such unimaginable things to you that you will wish I *had* killed you. Clyde will do it repeatedly until there is nothing left of your mind, until you are completely gone. Then he will kill you. But it won't be a quick death. Oh no, Clyde will draw it out so you feel you died a thousand times over. Then, and only then, will he let you die. Clyde won't just kill you, Liv; he will destroy you. And he will enjoy it." He exhaled a long, shaky breath.

Declan was so close, her breasts brushed against his chest as she sucked in a ragged breath. The smell of coffee

Chapter 7

and cigarettes surrounded her, and heat radiated from him. Olivia stared into his eyes.

"What happened to you, Declan?" she whispered. "What changed you into this ... this monster?"

Declan swallowed, his throat clicking. "Clyde killed my sister."

Olivia's heart twisted, and she gasped. She reached for Declan, but he took a step back, cleared his throat, and pinched the bridge of his nose.

"I'll give you an hour to get cleaned up." He spun around, grabbed his coat from the rack in the corner, and put it on as he yanked open the door and stepped outside.

Olivia watched Declan through the thin curtain covering the window. He leaned against the post on the porch with an unlit cigarette in his mouth and stared off into space. She glanced down the hallway toward the open bathroom door. She took one last look at the silhouette of her captor before she trudged down the hall to the bathroom.

Olivia locked the door behind herself. She immediately stripped out of her filthy clothes and tossed them in the sink. Her first instinct was to take a shower, make it as quick as possible, but Declan had given her an hour. If she took a bath, she could stretch it out, take advantage of every minute. Decision made, she turned on the water in the bathtub, running it as hot as she could handle.

As the tub filled, she washed her clothes in the sink, briskly rubbing them with the bar of soap she found on the edge of the tub. She didn't know what she was going to wear, but she couldn't stand another minute in the filthy garments. Once she had them as clean as she could get them with a bar of soap, she wrung them out and laid them out on the bathroom counter to dry.

When the tub was full, she eased into the hot water, hissing as her cold skin met the steaming water. She used the soap and a clean washcloth from under the sink to wash her body, then she scrubbed her greasy hair with the cheap shampoo she found. Once she was clean, she pulled her knees up to her chest, rested her forehead on them, and tried to relax.

Olivia couldn't stop thinking about what Declan said. She replayed the conversation in her head, picturing his face and the sound of his voice. In hindsight, she realized what had seemed menacing and evil was actually Declan's grief manifesting itself. She had felt a powerful urge to wrap her arms around him, hold him, and comfort him. They shared a common enemy; it was natural to want to comfort him.

Olivia shook herself free of those thoughts, refusing to acknowledge their existence. She refused to feel sorry for the man who held her hostage, despite their shared enemy and their shared romantic past.

She couldn't help but wonder if it was grief that had turned him, if it had changed him into the man he was now. Grief hardened a person, destroyed everything good about them. The Declan she remembered had been fun, crazy, a kid who lived on the edge and loved it. Nothing ever fazed him or bothered him. But she could see pain killing the man she had known.

Olivia had experienced that kind of pain while living with the Muldoons. She had to claw her way back from the edge and fought against it every day.

Chapter 7

The water cooled, causing goosebumps to rise on her skin. She squeezed the water from her hair, stepped out of the tub, and dried herself off as best she could. She secured the towel around her body, tucked the corner in between her breasts, and stepped out of the bathroom. Not finding Declan at first glance, she quickly snatched her dripping clothes, plus a spare towel, and then scurried to the bedroom that held her captive. She kept her eyes on the floor, intent on getting to the room.

While waiting for Declan's men to come back, she could use the quilt and towel to cover herself. She chastised herself, angry that she hadn't thought this through before deciding to wash her clothes in the sink. Not that she'd had much choice; she couldn't stay in those filthy clothes another minute.

She stepped through the door, shocked to see Declan beside the bed, a pile of sheets and blankets in his hands. Startled, Olivia let out a breathy squeak. Declan dropped the pile to the bed and swung around, his hand going to the gun tucked in his waistband.

Olivia froze, unable to move. She tightened her grip on the towel tucked between her breasts, shivering as water from the wet clothes dripped on her feet.

Declan released his hold on his weapon and stalked toward her. The sadness and grief were gone from his face; instead, the mask of a dangerous and menacing criminal was in its place. Gone was the vulnerable, grief-stricken man from earlier. Olivia didn't like the Declan standing before her right then.

Declan's eyes roamed over her body. "Nice look," he muttered.

Olivia opened her mouth to speak, but the front door slammed into the wall in the other room and jolted her into action. She darted around Declan, further into the room, out of sight of anyone entering the house.

"Put something on," he ordered. He pointed to the end of the bed where he had dropped the sheets and blankets, then he pulled the door closed. A few seconds later, the sound of men's laughter filled the other room.

Olivia hung her damp clothes on the bed's footboard, then she sorted through the bundle of items Declan had dropped. Clean sheets, another blanket, and thankfully, a clean shirt and a pair of dark blue sweatpants. The shirt was a light blue button down, obviously a man's shirt, well-worn but the fabric soft under her fingertips. She slipped it on and quickly buttoned it. The sleeves hung past her fingertips and the shirttail brushed the back of her thighs. The sweatpants were huge and barely stayed above her hips, even after she pulled the drawstring as tight as possible. At least it was something to wear.

Once she had dressed, Olivia perched on the edge of the bed and waited for Declan to return. She desperately wanted to talk to him. Maybe having a common enemy could benefit both of them.

Clyde Braniff might unite the mobster and his prisoner.

Chapter 8
Declan

Declan swallowed the rest of his coffee and stared at the bedroom door. Seeing Olivia again had stirred up emotions he'd held in check for eight years. He'd forgotten what it felt like to care about someone. Aside from his brother and Conor, he had no one. He liked it that way; Clyde couldn't take anyone else away from him.

His old feelings for Olivia rose to the surface when he talked to her. She'd always been fiery and determined to live her own life. He couldn't understand why she agreed to marry Clyde; it wasn't something the Olivia he had known would do. Of course, that had been eight years ago. People changed. But he'd glimpsed the woman he remembered when he'd held her against the wall and she'd fought with him.

He lit a cigarette and poured another cup of coffee from the pot. He checked his watch, saw that it was almost three in the morning, and wondered for the hundredth time if he could ever sleep again.

A floorboard squeaked on the other side of the bedroom door. A few seconds later, the knob twisted, and the door opened a few inches. Olivia peered out.

"Going somewhere?" he asked.

Olivia jumped, then opened the door all the way. "I thought you said there was nowhere to go," she muttered.

"There isn't." He smiled at her. "So, what are you doing?"

Olivia shrugged. "I couldn't sleep, so I checked the door on a whim. I didn't expect it to be unlocked. Are you angry?"

Declan shook his head and pointed at the chair across from him. "Sit down. I could use some company."

She took a step into the room, froze for a second and then darted back into the bedroom and returned with a blanket wrapped around her shoulders. She eased into the chair and stared at him.

Declan stabbed his cigarette out in an overflowing ashtray and took a sip of his coffee. "So, you couldn't sleep?"

"No," Olivia said. "I have bad dreams." She stared at the tabletop and traced a round coffee stain on the linoleum tabletop. "What about you?"

Declan shrugged. "I have bad dreams too."

Olivia stared at him, opened her mouth, and shut it again.

"What?" Declan asked.

"Tell me about your sister," she whispered. "Tell me what Clyde did to her."

Declan frowned. "You don't want to hear about that, Liv."

"I want to understand what changed you from the man I knew all those years ago to the man in front of me now. A man who terrifies people. Terrifies me. Tell me what happened, Declan. I need to know."

Declan sighed and shook his head. "Are you sure you want to hear this?" He waited for her to answer, but she just stared at him, waiting.

Chapter 8

"Somebody shot up Foley's Café two years ago, and I got injured," he explained.

"My father," Olivia interjected.

Declan nodded. "Thanks to Conor, I survived, but I fucked my leg up. I vowed to get out. No more mob shit. I didn't want to be a *girseach* anymore. Drew employed me as a private investigator, helping him to investigate cases from his law office. It was good and for the first time in a long time, I was happy."

"You weren't happy before?" Olivia asked.

"No surprise, but my mom and sister didn't like me working for the Muldoons. They hated it. I kept promising I would get out, especially after my mom died of cancer, but then I would make excuses not to leave. After I got hurt, I had no choice." Declan's hand shook as he lit another cigarette. "Things were good." He scratched the side of his nose with his finger and stared at a spot over her shoulder. "Drew handled some minor cases for a couple of Clyde's men. I helped. It impressed Clyde. He asked me to come work for him, full time. I declined. Clyde insisted, but I turned him down again. And again. Eventually, Drew dropped him and his men as a client, hoping he would back off."

"Did it work?" Olivia asked.

"We thought it did. Until three weeks later, when I came home, and my sister was gone. Two days later, Drew disappeared."

"I ... I don't understand," Olivia said, shaking her head.

Declan sucked in a deep breath. "Clyde took them. He promised they would go free if I did one job for him." He held up his index finger. "One job. A bank in Worcester. If I ... if I robbed it and got away clean, Clyde said he would release Drew and Sarah. That was it; one job. I figured it would be easy."

"But—," she prompted.

"Clyde got greedy," Declan explained. "One job became two, then three, and so on. He wouldn't stop. After the fourth or fifth job, when my name ended up on the front page of the newspaper, Twitter, Facebook, and all over the internet, I balked. I refused to do anymore. I told Clyde that I had reached my limit; I was done, and I demanded he bring my sister and brother back safely."

"What happened?"

Declan gnawed on his lower lip and stared into space. He opened his mouth, only to snap it shut again. He didn't know how to continue, how to get out the words. It was the first time he had talked about any of this with anyone. Conor didn't even know the complete story.

"That was when he killed Sarah," he whispered.

Olivia twisted her hands in her lap. "God, Declan, I'm so sorry."

Declan scrubbed a hand over his face. He refused to cry: it didn't help, it didn't solve anything, and it made him look and feel weak. He sat straight in his chair, shoulders back, fists clenched in front of him.

"Clyde took my family from me." He fumbled with the pack of cigarettes, somehow shook one out, and lit it with a shaking hand.

They sat in silence for several minutes, both lost in their own thoughts. Olivia poured herself a cup of coffee and sipped it slowly. She watched Declan carefully.

"Can I ask you a question?" she said. "You don't have to answer it if you don't want to."

"Go ahead," Declan said.

"I never met your sister. What was she like?"

Chapter 8

Declan smiled and dropped his cigarette in the ashtray, leaving it to burn itself out.

"Sarah was a handful," he said. "She was smart, funny, and she called me on my shit when I got out of hand. But she was also willful and determined to do her own thing. She had a full-ride scholarship to Boston University. Unfortunately, after Dad died and Mom got cancer, Sarah chose not to go. She thought she needed to stay home and take care of our mother. Both Drew and I tried to get her to go to school, but she insisted staying home was the right thing to do. She promised us she would go to school later when Mom was better. Except Mom died, and it sucked the life out of my sister. Sarah was finally coming around, thinking about going back to school when Clyde took her." He rubbed a hand over his face and grimaced. "When she was a little girl, she called me her hero. But I couldn't save her, not when it mattered most."

"I'm so sorry," Olivia whispered again. She shifted in her seat and stared at the table. "Is there a Mrs. Declan Quinn? Or a girlfriend maybe?"

Declan shook his head, surprised she'd asked such a forward question. "Nope." He smiled at her. "Nobody could replace you, Liv."

Olivia blushed. "That was a long time ago, Declan. You're telling me you haven't dated anyone in eight years?"

He laughed. "I didn't say I didn't date. But love? No. You're the only woman I've ever loved. In my own, fucked-up way. Aside from Conor, you were my best friend. When you disappeared from my life, I was at a loss."

That was another thing he'd told no one—how much he had loved Liv O'Reilly. When she'd stopped coming around, and Grady McCarthy told him to stay away from her, he hadn't known what to do or how to react. He shoved his feelings down deep inside himself and pretended they didn't exist. It was easier to cope that way.

"I didn't want to disappear, but my father—."

"He didn't approve of our relationship," Declan finished.

"Or your affiliation with the Muldoons. He wanted to protect me from them."

Declan's face hardened as he snarled at the thought of Olivia being forced to marry Clyde. "But he was okay with his daughter marrying one of them?"

Olivia pushed a hand through her hair. "It's complicated, Declan."

He shook his head. "It's not complicated. He sent his daughter to live with the enemy."

Olivia slapped her hands on the table. "Don't you think I know that? I live every day of my life knowing my father traded me for some kind of peace between the families. I'm not sure I can ever forgive him for that." She exhaled. "Look, if it hadn't been me, it would have been my sister. In fact, it was supposed to be my sister. Daddy was going to force Caitlin to marry Clyde. I wanted to protect my sister, so I offered to go in her place."

"Son of a bitch," Declan muttered.

"I told you, it's complicated." She rubbed her forehead, the ache behind her eyes coming out of nowhere. "I want to go home, Declan. I want to see my family. My mother and my sister. Except I can't go home because if I do, Clyde will kill me. But what scares me more than anything is that I don't know what my father will do to me for defying him. I don't think I will *ever* be able to go home."

Declan took her hands again and held them tight. "Maybe there's a way. You just have to find it."

Chapter 8

"It's too late for me. I threw everything away when I ran away. But you know what? I got out. I'm free." Olivia closed her eyes and chuckled. "Relatively speaking."

Declan chuckled. "I know, and I am sorry about that. I'm working on a way to fix that, I swear." He checked his watch. "Look, it's late, and we both need sleep. Why don't you go back to bed?"

He thought she might argue, but she rose to her feet, adjusted the blanket around her shoulders, and mumbled, "Good night." She stopped in the doorway, looked over her shoulder at him, her blue eyes flashing, and eased the door shut.

Chapter 9
Olivia

She lay on the bed, with all the blankets piled on her, and stared at the ceiling. She'd been counting the ceiling cracks for over an hour. Later, she thought she might try counting the tiny, pink flowers on the fading wallpaper again. When she'd tried yesterday, she'd fallen asleep and lost her place.

Day seven of her captivity was a wet, dreary day. Rain pounded the side of the house, and cold air slipped in through the window. The blankets didn't keep her warm.

She closed her eyes and pulled the blankets up to her ear. Maybe she would sleep. It was the only thing left to do in this hellhole. She wondered when, or even if, Declan planned to move on from this place. Not that she wanted him to; if Declan moved on from here, she wouldn't see him again. The thought of never seeing Declan Quinn again didn't sit well with her.

If Declan left, would he take her with him? Or would he leave her behind to fend for herself? Or maybe he would let one of his men take care of her. Olivia was confident that Walsh would be more than happy to eliminate her.

A sound like a gunshot echoed through the house, startling her out of a state of semi-consciousness. Olivia

Chapter 9

threw the blankets off and stumbled to her feet. It took her a second to realize that it wasn't a gunshot she'd heard but the door hitting the wall.

"Murphy, get the truck out of the barn!" Declan's voice reverberated through the walls, deep and gruff. "Conor, grab the guns from the back room. We're going to need them."

"There's some cash below the floorboards in the bathroom," Conor added. "Don't forget it."

Olivia ran to the window and watched Murphy run through the rain across the lawn to the barn, while the men shouted and caused a commotion in the house. He pushed open the enormous barn door and rushed inside. A few seconds later, a dark blue SUV emerged from the barn. He parked it in front of the house, jumped out, and ran around it, throwing open the doors.

The bedroom door flew open and hit the wall. Walsh came in and stalked toward her, his fists tightly clenched and an angry scowl on his face. Olivia pressed her back against the wall and put her hands up.

"Walsh!" Declan yelled. He ran into the room and darted between Walsh and Olivia, one hand on the gun under his arm. He scowled at Walsh, and Olivia swore she heard a low growl come from deep in Declan's chest. "Go help Murphy load the SUV. Now."

Walsh snarled at Olivia, then he abruptly turned and left.

Declan waited until Walsh went out the front door, then he kicked the door shut and turned back to her.

"Clyde is on his way back," he explained. "We have to go."

Olivia gasped. "What? Why?" Her stomach twisted, and she broke out in a cold sweat. "Why would he come back here?"

"I don't know, but I have my suspicions. That's why we have to leave." Declan grabbed the quilt from the bed and wrapped it around her. "Do not argue with me or fight with me. Do exactly as I say." He stared at her, waiting for her acknowledgement.

Olivia nodded. The flash of his gun beneath his coat reminded her who she was dealing with, despite their shared past and brief moments of bonding earlier in the night. At that moment, there was nothing of the sweet, kind person she'd known in the past and seen glimpses of the past few days. This was not the man she'd sat up late talking to about their mutual hatred of Clyde. This was Declan Quinn, the notorious mobster, bank robber, and alleged murderer. Declan scared her when he was like this.

Declan put a hand in the middle of her back and pushed her out the bedroom door in front of him. His men rushed around the house, gathering weapons and supplies. Through the open front door, she saw the dark blue SUV with its open doors. Parked behind it was a dark blue Mercedes. Declan pushed her through the house and ushered her down the porch steps. She flinched when her bare feet hit the wet, muddy ground. A rock pierced the bottom of her foot as she stepped into the dead grass. Afraid to utter a word of protest, she kept her mouth shut as Declan guided her across the dying lawn and shoved her into the backseat of the Mercedes. He climbed in beside her and pulled the door shut.

Olivia huddled in the backseat's corner and wrapped the quilt tight around herself. She gnawed on her lower lip and tried to ignore the pain from the cut pulsing in her foot.

Chapter 9

Conor climbed in the driver's seat and turned to look at Declan. "How long?" he asked.

Declan leaned over the front seat and checked his watch. "My guess? Thirty minutes."

"We can go," Conor said. "Walsh and Murphy can finish here."

"Then let's go," Declan said.

Conor nodded, started the car, and pulled away from the house. Olivia watched over her shoulder as the house disappeared behind her.

"Where are we going?" she asked.

As Declan sat back, his hand brushed against hers. He pulled his fedora down low and stared straight ahead.

"Albany," he replied. "I have a friend there who can help us."

"Help you do what?" she asked.

Declan looked at her out of the corner of his eye. He scrubbed a hand over his face.

"Hide."

It was dark after the four-hour drive to Albany when Conor parked the car in front of a large, two-story home in Albany, New York. Declan opened the door and stepped out while Conor kept the car running. He surveyed his surroundings before he leaned down and peered into the car. He held out his hand.

"Come on," he ordered.

Olivia gathered the quilt around her and slid across the seat. She hissed as her bare feet hit the cold concrete, and pain lanced through her injured foot. She glanced up and down the street, contemplating her chances of getting away.

Declan cleared his throat, drawing her attention back to him. He shook his head, a silent communication she immediately understood. He might as well have reached beneath his coat and pulled his gun from his holster. She nodded and followed him through a wrought-iron gate and up a steep set of stairs.

Declan pounded on the door as she shifted from foot to foot and shivered. She tried pulling the blanket tighter around herself, but it didn't do any good.

A tall, rail thin woman opened the door. She was older than either Olivia or Declan, with beautifully styled gray hair and dark pink lipstick. She wore a simple black dress and high heels, which only made her seem like she towered over them.

"Declan!" She smiled widely, then she pushed past them to look up and down the street. "Thank God! Get in here."

Declan didn't speak until they were in the foyer, with the door locked behind them. He stepped around Olivia, gathered the woman into his arms, hugged her close, and kissed her cheek.

"Thank you for this, Ezra. I know it puts you in danger—"

Ezra cut him off by grabbing his cheeks and squeezing. She shook her head and clicked her tongue. "Enough of that. You know I don't care about that." She tipped her head in Olivia's direction. "Is that her?"

"Yeah, that's her. Olivia. Do you have a place we can stash her?"

Red-hot irritation rushed through Olivia. She didn't take kindly to being treated like something that had to be hidden. For crying out loud, she was a living, breathing

Chapter 9

person. She kept her mouth shut and silently fumed. Speaking up wouldn't change anything.

"Declan." Ezra shook her head, but her protest died on her lips as Declan cut her off with nothing more than a look. Her mouth snapped closed, and she nodded.

"Conor is around back, putting the car in the garage," Declan explained. "Put Olivia somewhere. I need to go help Conor and make sure he's not seen. Walsh and Murphy will be here soon. They were right behind us." He glanced at Olivia before disappearing down a hallway that stretched out in front of them. A few seconds later, Olivia heard a door slam at the back of the house.

Ezra pointed at the stairs. "If you'll follow me, dearie." Her tone was sharp and curt, the endearment harsh and almost spiteful.

Olivia followed Ezra up two flights of stairs to the third floor, then they made their way down a long, narrow hallway. Her limp became more pronounced with each step, thanks to the cut on her foot. At the end of the hall, Ezra opened a door and turned on a lamp, the light spilling into the hallway.

Olivia peered around the older woman, curious to see where they would put her this time.

It was another bedroom, bigger than the one that had held her for the last week. There were more furnishings—a dresser, two bedside tables, a comfortable-looking chair, and, of course, the bed. But it was still nothing more than another locked room.

Declan's words echoed in her head. *Someplace to stash her.* When had her life become one of those parody-worthy soap operas? She pulled the quilt tighter around herself and gnawed at the inside of her cheek, determined not to cry. She took a tentative step into the room.

Out of nowhere, Ezra shoved Olivia, causing her feet to tangle, so she stumbled and fell to her knees just inside the room. Olivia dragged herself upright and glared over her shoulder at the woman in the doorway.

Ezra didn't offer an apology. She crossed her arms over her chest and glared at Olivia. "Are you fucking Declan or something? Or maybe Conor?" Her bitterness suggested she might have been jealous at the thought. "Or is it both? Is that it? You're fucking both of them?"

"No," Olivia snapped. "What kind of question is that? Do I look like I want to be here? Do you think I'm here of my accord, dressed in ill-fitting clothes that obviously aren't mine, hair a tangled mess, and blood dripping from my foot?" She dragged in a shaky breath. "Declan took me against my will, and now he's dragging me around, locking me up, and not telling me what he's going to do with me. I don't know from day to day if I'm going to live or die."

Ezra shrugged. "I figured you must be giving it up, or Declan would have offed you by now."

Anger flooded her. She rose to her feet, ignoring the pain in her heel. "Do you know who I am?" she asked.

"I don't care who you are," Ezra replied. "You are baggage. Dead weight. If you're not useful to Declan, he won't keep you around much longer. He doesn't have a reputation for being merciful. I'm sure you've heard the stories. Declan Quinn leaves death in his wake."

"You're not afraid of him," Olivia said.

"No, I'm not. But I'm useful to him." Ezra looked Olivia up and down. "I'll bring you some clothes." She pulled the door closed behind her and locked it.

As soon as the door shut, Olivia dropped the quilt to the floor and kicked it, an odd sense of satisfaction filling

Chapter 9

her when it crumpled against the wall. She stared at it for a long minute, then she limped across the room, picked it up, folded it, and laid it on the end of the bed.

After she was done, she shucked off the sweatpants, sat on the edge of the chair, and pulled her foot into her lap. There was a one inch cut on her heel with blood and dirt caked around it. She examined it, prodding at the skin around the cut. She didn't think she needed stitches, but it needed to be cleaned.

Olivia leaned her head against the back of the chair. Exhaustion wormed its way through every nerve ending. She looked out the window at the full moon. For the hundredth time in the last week, she tried to come up with a way out of her situation, but nothing came to mind.

It was time to talk to Declan; this couldn't go on any longer. Something had to give.

Chapter 10
Declan

Declan had just finished helping Conor get the car unloaded and into the garage when Walsh and Murphy arrived. They quickly unloaded the SUV, pulled it into the backyard, and threw a tarp over it. Once they were done, he crossed the yard and went through the back door into the kitchen. He slipped off his coat and dropped it on the back of a chair. After washing and drying his hands, he moved away as his men descended on the kitchen. He tossed the towel to Conor, who caught it deftly with one hand.

"You got a minute?" Declan asked Conor.

Conor nodded and followed Declan back through the house to the room Ezra called the library. He gestured to Conor to close the pocket doors while he poured two glasses of scotch. Once the doors were closed, he handed the drink to Conor.

"Did you talk to her?" Declan asked quietly.

Conor nodded. "She's in. According to her, Drew is being held by Clyde at the Muldoon compound. She thinks she can either get us in or maybe get him out. Either way, she'll do whatever we need." He took a sip of the scotch and cleared his throat. "Maybe we could talk

Chapter 10

to Olivia. She lived at the compound, Deck. She's familiar with the place. It's worth considering that she could be helpful to us."

Declan shook his head. "I don't want to put her in any more danger—."

"But you're okay with Ruthie putting herself in danger?" Conor snapped.

Declan sighed. "I didn't say that."

"It's implied."

Ruth Fraiser lived at the Muldoon compound, running the household. What Donovan Muldoon didn't know was that Ruth despised him and did everything she could to undermine him. Declan had been working with her for months, trying to get his brother out.

"Do me a favor and tell Ruthie to be careful. And that I said thank you," Declan said. "I know she's putting herself at risk, but the sooner we can get Drew out of that place, the sooner we can take off. You know as well as I do we can't hide here forever. It's not going to be long before Clyde wants to send us out on another job. I can only stall him for so long. And if Walsh talks to him—."

"We're done for," Conor finished. "Have you come up with an excuse to get rid of Walsh and Murph?"

"I think so," Declan said. "I'm going to send them to Ohio to scout the next job. By the time they figure out we aren't meeting up with them, we'll be long gone."

"So, we're gonna move fast," Conor said. "Get rid of Walsh and Murph, move in and get Drew, and disappear?"

Declan nodded.

"What about Olivia?" Conor asked. "And for Christ's sake, don't say 'I don't know' or I will kick your ass."

Declan downed his scotch. "I'm not letting her go."

"What?"

"I'm not letting her go," Declan repeated. "I can't protect her if she's not with me."

Conor sighed. "Are you sure?"

"No, I'm not sure of anything. I don't want to hold her hostage indefinitely, but if I let her go, I'm afraid Clyde will find her and kill her. I have no choice but to keep her close, to keep her safe." He'd considered releasing her, but the thought of Clyde finding her and hurting her held him back.

"This woman shouldn't matter," he silently chastised himself. In fact, he should run away from her, just knowing Olivia was dangerous. But he couldn't leave her.

The thought surprised him, even scared him a little. The only people in his life he gave a damn about were Conor and Drew. When did Olivia become one of those people?

"It's your call, boss," Conor said.

Declan rolled his eyes at Conor's sarcastic use of the word "boss." "Talk to Ruthie and formulate a plan to get Drew out. I trust the two of you to get it right."

The pocket doors opened, and Ezra entered, a stack of clothes under one arm. She nodded at Conor and Declan, then she grabbed a bottle of water from the top of the bar.

"I settled your guest in a room on the third floor," she said.

"Thank you. I really appreciate it," Declan said. "I can't tell you how much I appreciate your help, Ezra."

"Save it," Ezra snapped. She spun on her heel and left the room.

"Talk to Ruthie," Declan said. He refilled his glass from the bottle on the bar, then he followed Ezra down the hall. He caught up with her at the bottom of the stairs.

"Ezra? Are those for Olivia?"

Chapter 10

Ezra stopped on the third step, turned to look down at him, and nodded. "She can't stay in what she's wearing. They're so big on her, they're falling off. It's indecent. I found some of my sister's old clothes. It won't be a perfect fit, but it will cover her better than what she's wearing."

"I'll take them up," Declan said.

Ezra shook her head and sighed. "What are you doing, Declan?"

He stared up at her. "I don't know what you mean."

"What are you doing with that girl? Are you trying to get yourself killed?"

"I don't know what you're talking about," Declan said.

"I know who she is, Declan."

Declan narrowed his eyes. "What do you mean you know who she is?"

Ezra smirked. "She's Sean O'Reilly's daughter. Clyde Braniff's fiancée." When Declan opened his mouth to protest, she silenced him with one look. "Don't try to convince me she isn't. I lived and worked in Boston long enough to know what she looks like. Changing her hair color doesn't change her identity. Being with that woman is a bad idea. It's dangerous. I didn't think you were this stupid."

"I know what I'm doing," Declan said.

Ezra shook her head. "I don't think you do."

Declan went up the stairs, took the clothes from Ezra, and tucked them under his arm. "I'll take these to her. Do you have the key to the room?"

Ezra took the key out of the pocket in her dress and handed it to Declan.

"I've got everything under control, Ezra. I promise." He winked at her before he continued up the stairs.

Declan knocked on the bedroom door, but he was met with silence. He unlocked the door and pushed it open. Olivia sat in the chair by the side of the bed. The sweatpants were gone, and the blue button-down shirt she wore barely covered her thighs.

"I brought you some clothes," he said gruffly. He took a deep breath, tossed the clothes on the bed, and then took a drink from the glass of scotch in his hand. He forced himself to look away from her naked legs. That was when he noticed drops of blood on the hardwood floor.

He narrowed his eyes and took a step toward her, eyeing her up and down. There were several drops of blood on the floor. Looking closely, he noticed she wasn't putting any weight on one of her feet, and there was blood on the heel.

"Why is there blood on your foot?" he asked. He didn't wait for Olivia to answer; instead, he crossed the room and kneeled in front of her. He set his drink on the floor beside the chair, gently took her ankle, and examined her foot.

She tried to pull away from him. "It's fine," she muttered.

"It doesn't look fine," he snapped. He released her and pushed himself to his feet. "I'll be right back."

Declan disappeared out the door. He went into the bathroom down the hall, wet a washcloth from the cupboard, and grabbed the first aid kit from under the sink. Back in the bedroom, he pushed the door closed before he sat on the floor in front of Olivia and reached for her foot.

"I said it's fine," Olivia groused.

Chapter 10

Declan sighed and grabbed her ankle anyway. He propped her foot on his leg. He held it tight, not tight enough to hurt but enough so she couldn't pull free. "It needs to be cleaned and bandaged before it gets infected. I will not hurt you, Olivia."

"Fine," she grumbled. She stared at her hands and twisted them nervously in her lap.

Declan used the warm washcloth to clean the cut. She winced several times, but she didn't yank her foot out of his grip.

"You know what?" she asked.

"Hm?" Declan hummed.

"The irony of all this is that I went to nursing school."

Declan chuckled. "That is ironic." He cleared his throat. "Did you work as a nurse?" he asked.

Olivia shook her head. "For about a year. But when my father decided I was going to marry Clyde, he ordered me to give it up."

"Did that bother you?" Declan asked.

"Yes," Olivia said. "I had to give up something I loved to marry a monster. Of course, it bothered me."

Declan shook his head. "I'm sorry. It was stupid of me to ask."

"It's okay," she mumbled.

Declan set the washcloth on the floor and pulled a bandage from the first aid kit. "So, your father wanted to use his daughter to achieve peace between the families?"

Olivia closed her eyes. "I still remember my father summoning me and Caitlin to his office: the smell of his cigar, the sun shining on his desk, the jazz music playing from the stereo in the room's corner. I remember our mother in the chair beside me, smiling and nodding as my father talked to us. Caitlin kept bitching to him about being summoned to Daddy's office like one of his underlings. After listening to it for a few minutes, my father slammed his hand on his desk and told her to be quiet. I knew then something wasn't right."

"Is that when he said Caitlin was going to marry Clyde?" Declan asked.

Olivia laughed. "Oh no. He launched into some long, drawn-out speech about family obligations and our responsibilities as his children. Blah, blah, blah." She exhaled. "When Daddy said the war between the Muldoons and the O'Reillys had gone on long enough, I knew what was coming. I don't know how, but I did."

Declan sat back on his haunches. "You knew your father was going to make Caitlin marry Clyde?"

"No, honestly, I thought it was going to be me. But Daddy threw a curveball. When he announced we were going to help unite the families by marrying the heir to the Muldoon fortune, I assumed it would be me. When he said it was Caitlin, I almost fell out of my chair."

Declan shook his head. "Why Caitlin and not you? You're the oldest."

"Caitlin is stubborn and strong-willed. I think Daddy thought she was a better match for Clyde than I was, that she could hold her own against him. But I couldn't let that happen. So, I offered to go in her place."

"How did Caitlin feel about that?" Declan asked.

Olivia shrugged. "Relieved and pissed at the same time. Not that there was much she could do about it. Daddy was so proud of me for stepping up and agreeing to do the right thing."

Declan removed all the blood from her foot as she talked, then he wrapped the bandage around her wounded foot and taped it in place. When he was done, he patted

Chapter 10

her leg and rose to his feet with his drink in hand. He swallowed the last of it and set the glass on the bureau.

"Why does Clyde want you back so bad? Did he fall in love with you or something?" The thought made Declan want to kill the little shit.

Olivia snorted. "No. It took both my father and Donovan Muldoon to convince Clyde to marry me. To sweeten the deal, he offered Muldoon a four-million-dollar dowry. Two million when we got engaged and another two million to be delivered after we said our vows."

"Clyde doesn't want you," Declan said. "He wants the rest of the money."

Olivia stared at him. She opened her mouth, then snapped it shut.

Declan sat on the edge of the bed. "What? What is it, Liv?"

Olivia lowered her voice until it was a low whisper. "I … I took the money, Declan. My father put the money in a joint account in both of our names, mine and Clyde's. Before I left, I emptied the account and transferred all the money to an overseas account under the Olivia Miller name. It vanished overnight."

"Jesus Christ," Declan muttered. "You stole the money?"

Olivia nodded. "He wants me dead, and he wants the money. Those are the only two things that matter to him. That's why I can't go home as much as I might want to. He won't hesitate to kill me."

"Olivia—."

"If you let me go, I'll give you half the money," she blurted. She got to her feet and stood in front of him, wobbling slightly. "Let me go and it's yours. I'll disappear and you'll never hear from me again, but you'll be a million dollars richer. All you have to do is turn your back long enough for me to leave. I'm safer on my own."

Declan shook his head and rose to his feet. "Absolutely not. I can't protect you if I let you go."

"What?"

"Don't you understand?" He took her arm and held it tight. "I want to keep you safe, Liv. I *need* to keep you safe. But I can only do that if you're with me."

"What do you mean you need to keep me safe?"

Declan realized he was still in love with Olivia after all this time. Overcome with emotion, he wrapped an arm around her waist and rested his forehead against hers. "I love you. I never stopped loving you. And now, by some crazy act of God, you drop back into my life, and I have a chance to do it over. The right way this time. I won't let anyone come between us. You are mine, Liv O'Reilly. I will protect you no matter what."

He ducked his head and caught her lips in his, as Olivia pushed up on her toes to meet him. His heart pounded as the kiss deepened. It had been too long since he'd tasted her lips and held her in his arms. He wouldn't let her get away again.

Declan released her and took a step back to calm down. "I better get back downstairs. I need to get Murphy and Walsh on the road."

Olivia nodded. "Thank you for taking care of my foot," she whispered breathlessly.

"You're welcome," he replied. He brushed a kiss across her lips.

The door flew open, and Conor darted inside. "Deck, it's Drew. He's here, downstairs. He's beat to shit, but he's alive."

Chapter 11
Olivia

Olivia dressed quickly, even though the clothes Declan brought her were too big and the undergarments were too small. The shoes were the right size, though hideously ugly: the color of dirt and chunky with a thick heel, squared-off toes, and a large, gold buckle across the top. Olivia would have to make do with what they had given her.

After dressing herself, Olivia perched on the edge of the bed, twisted her hands in her lap, and stared at the door. After a few minutes, she pushed herself to her feet and crossed the room. She opened the door a few inches and listened. Voices rose from the floor below, faint, indiscernible. Olivia stepped into the hall, turned around, and put her palm flat against the door. She eased it closed without making a sound, then she walked down the corridor, slowly, pausing every few feet to listen. She reached the bottom of the first set of stairs and listened, making sure that she hadn't been heard and that the murmur of voices remained the same. When she was confident that no one was coming, she continued down the second flight of stairs to the foyer.

"We need to do something!" Declan yelled from the back of the house.

Declan's voice sent a chill rushing through her, and she froze as goosebumps rose on her skin. Olivia exhaled and hurried down the remaining stairs. At the bottom of the stairs, she paused and listened. Voices came from the back of the house. Olivia headed down the hall, letting some marrow-deep instinct pull her to a library-like room in the middle of the house. She stopped outside the door and peered into the room.

Declan's men had gathered in a rough half-circle around a long sofa. Ezra and Declan kneeled on the floor beside it where a tall, gaunt man in his late twenties laid. Despite his battered appearance, Olivia recognized him immediately. It was Drew, the man she'd seen with Clyde. Declan's brother.

Conor hadn't been exaggerating when he said Drew was beat to shit. Drew's face was swollen twice its size, and it looked purple and grotesque. A cut split his lip in two places, and there was a cut above his eyebrow that wouldn't heal without stitches. Every few seconds, he would groan loudly.

The men in the room stared helplessly at one another, obviously unsure of what to do. Declan and Ezra appeared to be trying to help; he checked Drew's wounds while Ezra frantically wiped away the copious amounts of blood smeared across Drew's face.

Olivia took a deep breath and stepped into the room. Only one man noticed her and, of course, it was the one who hated her the most. Walsh pulled his gun from its holster and pointed it at her, an angry scowl on his face. Olivia flinched, but she stood her ground.

Chapter 11

"What the hell are you doing down here?" Walsh demanded. The other men in the room turned to look at her.

Olivia ignored Walsh and the gun he had pointed at her face. She focused on Declan and his brother, pushed past the men surrounding them, and crouched between Declan and Ezra. She put a hand on Declan's arm.

"I can help him," she whispered, close to his ear.

"Wh-what?" Declan was confused and agitated. He blinked several times before he looked at Olivia, as if he'd never seen her before. "How can you help him?"

"I told you I was a nurse." Olivia swallowed the lump of fear rising in her throat. "Remember how I said I went to nursing school and worked as a nurse for a year?" She glanced at the other men staring intently at her. Olivia didn't know what these men knew about her and her past, so she was vague. "Before ... before I met my husband."

"Oh, for the love of Christ." Walsh still had his gun out, though he'd lowered the weapon and held it at his side. Now, he stalked across the room, grabbed Olivia's arm, and yanked her to her feet.

Something flickered in Declan's eyes—anger and maybe hope. He straightened his shoulders and glared at Walsh. "Shut up, Walsh," Declan snapped. "Put your damn gun away and let go of her."

When Walsh hesitated, Declan jumped to his feet and grabbed the man's wrist. His fingers trembled, but his voice was darkly threatening. "I said put it away and let her go. Now."

Walsh yanked his arm free, released her, and glared at Declan and then Olivia. He huffed loudly and stalked away from the room. A few seconds later, a door at the back of the house slammed shut.

Declan turned to Olivia and pointed at the man on the sofa. "Help my brother."

Drew muttered, "thank you," to Olivia before he drifted off to sleep. She didn't move, choosing to stay with him so she could watch over him. She also needed a minute to catch her breath.

Olivia hadn't used her nursing skills since a year after college. After escaping the Muldoon compound, she decided it would be best if she didn't work as a nurse. It would be too hard to keep her certificate current or even get credentials.

A quiet moan came from the man in the bed, pulling her from her thoughts. She got up to check on him, but he was asleep, out cold, thanks to the half-bottle of whiskey his brother forced down his throat; it was the only sedative available. Olivia brushed Drew's long hair off his forehead, then she returned to her seat.

Drew's appearance improved after they cleaned the blood off his face and stitched the cut above his eye. She still couldn't believe she'd stitched him up cleanly; it had taken two shots of whiskey for her and Declan and Conor to hold Drew down while she worked. She'd bit her lip raw, and tears had run down her cheeks as Drew screamed and moaned while she worked. Intense relief flooded her when she finally dropped the needle on the table.

Declan helped her dress Drew's ribs as he grumbled. Then they got him out of his soiled garments and into something clean. Afterward, Declan and Conor took Drew to a bedroom on the second floor.

Chapter 11

Declan excused himself shortly after they got Drew settled, leaving Olivia to sit with Drew. She was relieved to see him go. He was a bundle of nerves: on edge, pacing and hovering, the anger rolling off him in waves. He tried to question Drew, ask him what happened, and how he'd gotten to Ezra's, but Drew was too exhausted and in too much pain. When his brother couldn't answer, a frustrated Declan walked out, slamming the door of the second-story bedroom shut behind himself.

Declan was gone two hours before he returned to the house. He stepped into the room with a determined look on his face, hat pulled down low over his eyes, coat buttoned to his chin, and an expensive bottle of whiskey clutched in one hand. He strode past Olivia and went directly to his brother. Without turning around, he spoke.

"You can go, Olivia. Thank you for your help." His cold, distant voice scared her.

"It's alright, I can stay with him," she said. "I can stay with *you*."

"I said you can go," Declan repeated. "Conor is waiting in the hall to escort you to your room. Thank you for helping my brother."

Olivia rose to her feet and moved to the bed to stand beside Declan. Her shoulder brushed his arm as she leaned around him to check on Drew. She adjusted one bandage and tucked his hair behind his ear.

She turned to Declan and put her hand on his arm. "Don't shut me out, Declan. Let me help you." She kissed his cheek and left.

Conor waited in the hall, just as Declan said he would be. He gestured for her to go in front of him and followed her up the stairs to the third floor. He stood aside as she stepped into the room, mumbled, "Good night," then he closed the door behind her.

Olivia stood in the center of the room, tense and uncomfortable thanks to the anger and frustration rushing through her. She glanced at the clock on the bedside table: 2 a.m. Sleep was what she needed.

She went through the pile of clothes from Ezra, looking for something to wear to bed. The nightgown she found was pale pink, oversized, and looked like it belonged to her eighty-year-old grandmother. She tossed it aside, undressed, and slipped on the pale blue shirt Declan had given her.

Olivia climbed into bed and turned off the light. She thought she might have trouble falling asleep, but she'd barely pulled the blankets up to her chin before she dozed off.

Chapter 12
Declan

After escorting Olivia to her room, Conor returned to Drew's room. He stepped inside, shut the door, and leaned against it with his arms crossed. Declan turned to look at him.

"Is he awake yet?" he asked, tipping his head in Drew's direction.

Declan shook his head. "Not yet. That half-bottle of whiskey knocked him out."

Conor shifted from one foot to the other. "Are you thinking what I'm thinking?"

Declan finally looked at his best friend. "That this feels like a trap? Yeah, I am." He rubbed the back of his neck. "Clyde could have let Drew go to draw us out. Did you get a hold of Ruth?"

Conor shook his head. "She's not answering my texts."

"Shit," Declan grumbled.

"Shit is right," Conor agreed. "I'm worried about her."

Drew groaned and rolled to his side, so Declan stepped away from the side of the bed and went to stand next to Conor.

"Maybe Drew just escaped," Declan whispered. "I mean, it looks like he was in one hell of a fight. It could have happened while he was getting out of the compound."

Conor grimaced. "I need to talk to Ruth. She'll know what happened."

"Keep trying," Declan said. "We need to know if she's okay and if she knows anything about Drew."

Conor nodded. "I'm trying every five minutes." He stifled a yawn. "I'm dragging, bro. I'm gonna crash for a couple of hours. Are you okay?"

"Yeah. I'll stay in here with Drew."

Conor clapped him on the shoulder, opened the door, and stepped out. Declan shut it behind, then he dropped into the chair next to the bed.

Resting his head against the back of the chair, he closed his eyes. He found it difficult to send Olivia to her room, but he couldn't have her around as a distraction. He had to figure out how his brother got away from Clyde. The mobster had been holding his brother for more than a year, using him as leverage to get what he wanted out of Declan. Were Drew's injuries a message? Or had Drew gotten hurt while attempting to escape?

Declan watched his little brother sleep, wishing he would wake up so he could get the answers he needed. His thoughts drifted to the woman upstairs; as much as he wanted to pretend she wasn't a distraction, she had gotten under his skin again.

His eyes slipped closed. Declan could see her clearly, like a photo on the back of his eyelids—her dark brown hair, her blue eyes, and the dusting of freckles on her nose. She looked more like the Olivia he remembered now that she didn't have her colored contacts or makeup to hide the freckles.

Chapter 12

She was more beautiful than he remembered. God, he had been so desperately in love with her. But it was more than her beauty that had drawn him to her; she was strong-willed, but with an aura of vulnerability that appealed to him. Beautiful, strong, and vulnerable in one package.

Olivia was also the daughter of a man he considered an enemy. All his life, he'd run with the Muldoons. His father had been what they called *forneart*, an enforcer. Seamus Quinn worked for the Muldoons his entire life. Since his childhood, his father taught Declan to loathe individuals affiliated with the O'Reillys.

Declan didn't know Olivia was an O'Reilly when they met. All he knew was she was a pretty girl eating French fries at Folger's Café. He flirted with her, she blushed but flirted back, and the next thing he knew, they were spending every second together. During the weeks that followed, Declan fell hard and fast and was pretty sure the same was true for Olivia.

He was so far gone that even finding out she was the daughter of Sean O'Reilly didn't change his feelings. The secrecy of their relationship only made it more appealing, especially for Olivia. At nineteen, she was determined to defy her father. It was one more thing he loved about her.

Then, one day, Olivia disappeared. She stopped coming around Folger's and didn't return his calls. Grady McCarthy showed up and told Declan to stay away from Olivia. Since he couldn't exactly march into the O'Reilly mansion and drag her out of there, he mourned the loss of his first love and tried to move on.

Drew groaned, interrupting Declan's musings. Drew had curled himself into a ball with his knees drawn up and his arms wrapped around his chest. A grimace of pain crossed his face, even in sleep.

Declan turned off the lamp on the bedside table and picked up the bottle of whiskey he brought with him. He would wait for Drew to wake up to get answers to the questions only he could answer. And he would try not to think about the woman in the bedroom upstairs.

"Deck? Declan?"

Declan twisted in the chair and kicked over the empty whiskey bottle at his feet. He opened his eyes to see Drew staring at him. His brother tried to smile, though it wasn't easy with his split lip.

"Hey, big brother," Drew mumbled.

"You're awake," Declan said. He pushed himself upright. "How are you feeling?"

Drew chuckled, wincing when it obviously hurt. "Like shit," he replied. "Who fixed me up?"

Declan ignored the question. "Are you hungry? Thirsty?"

Drew nodded. "I would love some water. And do you have anything for the pain? Anything at all?"

"I'm sure Ezra's got something around here. I'll go find it." He shoved himself out of the chair. "Anything else?"

Drew gingerly touched the stitches on his forehead. "Who fixed me up, Deck?"

"I'll explain, I promise. Let me get you some food and pain meds. Then we'll talk. I have questions for you too."

Everybody was awake and in the kitchen. Walsh sat at the table, checking something on his phone; Murphy leaned against the counter drinking coffee; and Conor was at the sink, washing dishes.

Chapter 12

"Did Ezra put you to work?" Declan asked.

Conor laughed. "Yeah. Is Drew awake?"

"Awake, hungry, thirsty, and in pain."

"We've got eggs, toast, and coffee," Conor said. "I'll ask Ezra if she's got pain meds."

"Did anybody take Olivia something to eat?"

Conor nodded. "Ezra did."

"Do me a favor," Declan said. "Bring her to Drew's room in about twenty minutes."

"Will do, boss," Conor replied.

Declan turned to Walsh and Murphy. "I want the two of you to spend some time checking small towns in Ohio. That's where we're headed next. Find me our next job."

Murphy straightened up. "We're gonna do another job?"

"Yeah, we are. Find me a place in Ohio. I want an answer by the end of the day." Declan grabbed a plate, loaded it with food, then took two bottles of water from the fridge. "Twenty minutes, Conor."

Back upstairs, Declan coaxed Drew into eating the eggs and a few bites of toast. He downed the water and asked for more. Declan waited until his brother had eaten before he started asking questions.

"How'd you get out?" Declan asked.

Drew took a sip of water. "Ruth. She put me in the back of a delivery truck. I got to downtown Boston and then hitchhiked my way here. There was nowhere else I could think of going. I knew Ezra would help me."

"Who beat the shit out of you?"

"Clyde's men." Drew shifted in the bed, grimacing in pain as he did. "It was supposed to be a message to you."

"A message?" Declan said.

Drew nodded. "Yeah. When they showed up at the safe house and you weren't there, I guess Clyde lost his mind. He had a couple of his goons take me down to the stables and beat the shit out of me. They took a bunch of pictures with their phones, said Clyde would send them to you. When Ruth got a look at me, she helped me get out. She said she couldn't stand by any longer while Clyde destroyed another family."

"Does Clyde know Ruthie helped you?" Declan asked.

"I don't think so," Drew replied. "God, I hope he doesn't. I couldn't handle it if he hurt her. She's a good woman, Deck."

Declan nodded. "I know. She's invaluable."

"When are you going to answer my question?" Drew asked. "Who fixed me up?"

Before Declan could answer, there was a light tap on the door, and Olivia entered with Conor right behind her.

Drew smiled as best he could with his split lip. "Conor. It's good to see you."

"You too," Conor replied. "From Ezra." He tossed a bottle of pain pills on the bed. "You look like shit."

Drew chuckled. "Thanks."

"We'll catch up later, kid. I'll see you." Conor excused himself, leaving Drew, Declan, and Olivia to stare at each other.

Drew broke the uncomfortable silence first. He nodded at Olivia. "Who is this?"

"This is Olivia," Declan said. "She fixed you up. Olivia, this is my brother, Andrew."

"Thank you," Drew said. "And call me Drew."

"You're welcome." She glanced at Declan. "Can I check his bandages?"

Declan nodded. "Go ahead."

Olivia straightened her shoulders and crossed the room to stand beside Drew. She checked his bandages

Chapter 12

and examined the uncovered wounds. Declan leaned against the wall by the door, watching every move she made and waiting patiently for her to finish.

"Have you eaten anything?" she asked.

"Yes," Drew replied. "Some eggs and toast. I also drank some water."

"Good." She cleared her throat and stepped away from the bed.

"I'm sorry, but you look really familiar," Drew said. "Do I know you?"

Olivia glanced at Declan. He shook his head. He didn't know if Drew even remembered Olivia, and he wasn't ready to reveal her secret to anyone else. It was enough that he and Conor knew. No one else needed to know whose daughter she was.

"I ... I don't think so," she mumbled. She scooted away and perched on the edge of the chair.

Drew looked at his brother and Olivia. Declan knew Drew didn't believe her, but he wouldn't pursue an answer, not if he thought Declan didn't want him to ask questions. After growing up the way they did, Drew knew when to keep his mouth shut.

Declan gestured to Olivia. "Come on. I'll walk you back to your room."

She smiled at Drew, got up, and followed Declan out the door. She walked quietly behind him back upstairs and went into the bedroom without a word.

Declan stepped inside and closed the door. He caught Olivia's hand and dragged her into his arms. He kissed the top of her head.

"I'm sorry about earlier. I shouldn't have shut you out." He hugged her tightly. "You have to understand something about me. I have lost everyone I care about in this world, except my brother. My go-to defense is silence. I'm not always good with words, Liv. Can you forgive me?"

Olivia nodded. She pressed her face against his chest and returned the hug. "Don't do it again, though, okay? I'm not going to sit by and blindly take orders from you. If I'm going to stay, you need to understand we are in this together."

"I won't do it again. I promise." He kissed her and for the first time since Drew showed up, Declan thought things might be okay.

Chapter 13
Olivia

Olivia pushed her tangled hair off her face, sat up, and turned on the bedside lamp; it didn't do much to illuminate the room. She checked her watch and saw that it was almost 10 p.m.; it had been hours since she had seen anyone. After Declan left her room, she slept for a couple of hours, tossing and turning the entire time. She was awake when Ezra marched in around four in the afternoon, set food on the bureau, and left without a word.

After she ate, she paced around the room and stared at the ceiling and the floor. She went through the dresser and the closet, though she didn't know what she was looking for in either place. She knew she was sick of doing nothing. Olivia wasn't an idle person: she liked to read, do yoga, and jog. She had also gotten invested in a couple of shows on one of the streaming services. Being locked in a room with nothing to do made her feel like her brain was rotting.

Olivia stood up, took two steps to the window, and pushed the curtain aside. The darkness outside was so thick that it seemed like an eerie, odd blackness had taken over the world. She let the curtain fall back into place, then she tiptoed across the floor and pressed her ear to the door.

Silence.

She sighed. Sitting was unbearable, so she paced around in circles instead. She was restless, irritated, and trapped. She wanted to scream.

Olivia paced for almost an hour before she heard a knock on the door. It opened, and Declan stepped into the room.

He had a cigarette between his fingers and a glass of scotch in his hand. "You're awake."

"I am." She cleared her throat. "How is your brother?"

"He's okay," Declan said. "Tired. Sore. But he'll live. Thanks to you." He took another step into the room and pointed at the chair. "Do you mind if I sit?"

Olivia shook her head. "No." She perched on the edge of the bed and folded her hands in her lap. "And you? How are you?"

Declan shrugged. "I'm exhausted."

"I'm sure you are," Olivia murmured.

"What about you?" Declan asked. "Can't sleep?"

Olivia snorted. "I've slept too much. I'm going stir crazy being trapped in one small bedroom after another." She stared at Declan.

He scrubbed a hand over his face. "I'm sorry about that. I really am." He downed the amber liquid in the glass, set it on the floor, and dropped his cigarette in the glass. "Murphy and Walsh make me uneasy when they're around you. Especially Walsh. If he finds out who you are, I guarantee you he will tell Clyde."

Olivia believed him; he seemed genuinely sorry. "But isn't Walsh one of your men? Wouldn't he be loyal to you?"

Declan shook his head. "No. Murphy isn't one of my guys either. Clyde put them with me, promised they'd follow orders, and do as they were told. I don't think

Chapter 13

Murphy will do anything, but since they both work for Clyde, I can't guarantee their loyalty."

"That's why you're keeping me locked up?" she asked.

"The door isn't locked. You can come out any time you want," Declan said. "Walsh doesn't know that, though." Declan cleared his throat. "I told you why we left the safe house so suddenly, right?" he asked. "Because Clyde was on his way back?"

"Yes," Olivia replied.

"There was no explanation or reason why Clyde was on his way to the safe house, just a phone call from one of his men telling us to expect him. I think … I think he knew our hostage was alive."

Olivia swallowed and rubbed her forehead. Her head hurt. "Oh, God," she groaned.

"I don't think he knew it was you, Liv. But he knew our hostage was alive. And he was coming back to take care of it."

"How did he find out?" she whispered.

Declan stared at the door. "I think Walsh told him."

Olivia nodded, though she wasn't really listening. She was trying to decide whether she should run. Even though Declan had promised to protect her, she didn't think he could save her from Clyde. No one could.

"You need to let me go," she blurted. "Let me leave. You know I won't talk. But if Clyde finds me—." A tear ran down her cheek, and she trembled.

He can't find me.

"Liv, it's okay," Declan said.

Olivia jumped to her feet, wincing when her injured foot hit the floor. "No, it's not. It is most definitely *not* okay. You don't understand, Declan. Clyde will kill me. And not just because I took the money." She sucked in a deep breath. "I defied him. As far as he is concerned, I belong to him, and he will stop at nothing to possess me again. That is all I am to him. A possession. A possession he lost and wants back." She looked out the window, then turned back to Declan. "Let me go, Declan. Please?"

She moved toward the door, but before she reached it, Declan grabbed her, one hand on her hip and his arm around her waist. She spun around to face him. Her heart pounded in her chest, hard enough to hurt. She put her hands on his chest and pushed, desperate to get away.

"Liv, stop," he whispered. "I won't hurt you." He swallowed, his throat clicking. "I know you're afraid of Clyde, but if you let me, I can protect you. I swear I can keep you safe."

Declan slid his hand up her body and around her throat until his hand rested under her chin. He tipped her head back and brushed a kiss across her lips. It was gentle, seeking something from her she desperately wanted to give him.

"What is it about you, Liv?" he asked. He caressed her cheek with the tip of his finger. "How come it was so easy to fall back in love with you?"

Olivia couldn't answer him. She didn't understand what was happening. After all these years, Olivia couldn't help but feel drawn to Declan Quinn, and she didn't understand why. What she knew was that she didn't want it to stop. She couldn't leave Declan. He had her under his spell.

Olivia took his hand and intertwined her fingers with his. She pulled his arm around her waist and stepped close, her body flush against his.

Declan traced a finger down her throat, over the center of her chest, and back. His hand closed around her throat again and her mouth fell open, inviting him

Chapter 13

to kiss her. This kiss was deeper, more intense than the first. It was Declan claiming her as his, his way of letting her know he wanted her. His tongue slid into her mouth and danced across her teeth. His sigh mingled with hers.

Heat spread through Olivia, and a tingle of desire exploded through every one of her nerve endings. She wrapped both arms around Declan and pushed herself up and into the kiss. She closed her eyes and let herself go.

Declan pulled away first and took a step back. "I'm sorry," he whispered.

Olivia shook her head. "Don't. Don't take this away from me by apologizing. This is something we both want, something we've both wanted for a long, long time. Don't minimize it with half-hearted apologies."

He brushed a hand down her cheek and smiled, the first genuine smile Olivia had seen on his face since he'd taken her from the bank. "No apologies. But I need to go. I need to get Drew some food and water." Declan pulled her into his arms, kissed her cheek, and left. He didn't lock the door behind him.

Olivia felt oddly sick to her stomach and strangely excited at the same time. It thrilled her to reconnect with Declan, but she was still afraid of him. He wasn't the same person she had known all those years ago. The death of his sister broke him, changed him, and turned him into a mobster that people were terrified of crossing. She knew she had to be careful.

Her world had spun out of control, and there was no way of stopping it.

Chapter 14
Declan

Declan went downstairs after leaving Olivia. As exhausted as he was, he wasn't sure he could sleep, so he decided another drink might help him relax. He made his way through the silent house and into the kitchen. After pouring a drink, he went out the back door. He stood on the porch, shivering as the chilly night air surrounded him. He scrubbed a hand over his face and grimaced at the gritty feeling in his eyes.

What the hell am I doing?

Declan sank to the top step on the porch, his elbows on his knees. He slid a cigarette out of the pack in his pocket, lit it, and took a slow drag, squinting as the icy breeze blew the smoke into his eyes. He pinched the bridge of his nose and shook his head.

Falling for Olivia wasn't part of the plan. In fact, it didn't figure into his plan at all. Since he was close to finishing things with Clyde, he needed to stay focused and not let Olivia distract him. With his brother safe, Clyde had nothing left to hold over him. Nothing would keep Declan from destroying him.

Unless he finds out about Liv.

Chapter 14

Declan chastised himself for his stupidity. He'd put Olivia in danger. If Clyde discovered Declan had feelings for her, it would only make him more desperate to kill her. Declan couldn't decide whether he should keep Olivia by his side to protect her or send her away to ensure her safety. Neither option seemed like a good one.

He meant it when he said he wanted to protect her. Olivia had to be kept safe from harm. Which meant keeping her away from Clyde and the inevitable danger he presented. Declan hadn't been able to protect his sister or his brother, but he would protect Olivia.

"With my life," he vowed.

Declan slept like shit, tossing and turning all night. He gave up around six, climbed off the bed, and made his way downstairs to the kitchen.

Walsh was at the table with his phone in his hand. As soon as Declan walked into the room, he dropped it face down on the table.

"Uh, hey, Deck," he said. "You sleep okay?"

"No," Declan grumbled. "What are you doing?"

Walsh shrugged. "Oh, I was, uh, just checking last night's basketball scores. I put some cash on the college games."

Declan narrowed his eyes. "You put money on the games? With who?" If Walsh called Muldoon's bookie to put money on the games, Clyde would find them.

Walsh's eyes widened. He shook his head and snatched his phone off the table. "I used one of those betting apps," he explained.

Declan's shoulders relaxed and the tension in his neck eased. "Okay." He exhaled. "March Madness, right? Any upsets?"

Walsh's eyes darted left, then back to Declan. "Uh, no, I don't think so."

Declan grabbed a cup from the cupboard and filled it with coffee from the pot by the stove. He searched the cupboards for something to stave off the headache pounding behind his eyes. "Is there any goddamn aspirin in this place?"

Walsh jumped out of his chair. "I think I saw some in the bathroom. I'll get it." He disappeared down the hall. He returned a minute later and set a bottle of aspirin on the counter.

"Thanks," Declan mumbled. "Where is everybody?"

"Ezra went shopping," Walsh explained. "She said something about five grown men in the house requiring more food. I think Conor and Murph are still asleep."

Declan shook two pills out of the bottle and downed them with his coffee, wincing when it burned his tongue. He sat down across the table from Walsh.

"Did you and Murph find anything in Ohio?" he asked.

Walsh nodded. "We found a couple of places. They need to be scouted, but they look like potential marks." He shifted in his chair and stared at the tabletop. "How much longer are we going to stay here?"

"I don't know," Declan replied. "Why?"

"Are we staying because of the girl?"

"You need to mind your business and stay away from the girl," Declan snapped.

Walsh snorted. "That's what Conor said."

"Conor is smart," Declan said. "You should listen to him."

Chapter 14

"You know, I could take care of her. I'll make it quick and painless. I'll take her out in the middle of nowhere—."

Declan slammed his hand on the table so hard that his coffee sloshed over the side of the cup. "Enough. You will not touch her. You will go nowhere near her. Do you understand me?"

Walsh sat back and crossed his arms over his chest. "Sure, boss. Whatever you say."

Declan shoved himself out of the chair, coffee in hand, and went upstairs. He checked on Drew, who was still asleep, and made his way to the third floor to Olivia's room. He tapped twice before opening the door and stepping inside.

Olivia paced the small room, wrapped in a blanket. She stopped when he came in.

"Hi," she murmured.

"Hey there," he said. "Did you get any sleep?"

She nodded. "A little."

"Are you okay?" he asked. He knew it was a stupid question; she was being held against her will in a strange town by a bunch of thugs. But after last night and the kiss they'd shared, as well as the things they'd talked about, he needed to know.

"I'm okay," she said. "I'm sick of being cooped up."

"Would you like to go for a walk? Outside?"

A smile spread across Olivia's face. "I would love that," she whispered.

"Get dressed and come downstairs. I'll be in the kitchen."

Declan stepped out of the room and pulled the door closed behind him. He jogged down to his second-floor bedroom and put on jeans and a long-sleeved Henley, along with boots and a jacket. He tucked his gun in the waistband of his jeans and went downstairs.

Conor and Murphy had gotten up while he was upstairs. The men were in the kitchen with Ezra, drinking coffee and eating fresh pastries at the kitchen table.

"Morning, boss," Conor said. "Is Drew awake? Does he want something to eat?"

Declan shook his head. "He's still asleep." He took a deep breath. "Olivia is coming down. I'm going to take her outside for some fresh air."

Murphy squirmed in his chair and Walsh made a face. He opened his mouth to say something, but Declan silenced him with one look. Ezra cleared her throat and shook her head.

Declan checked his watch, poured himself another cup of coffee, and ignored the disapproving looks aimed at him from the other people in the room. He leaned against the kitchen counter to wait for Olivia. Conor rose to his feet and sauntered across the room; it did not surprise Declan that it was his best friend who spoke up.

"What are you doing, Deck?" Conor whispered.

Declan sipped his coffee and raised an eyebrow. "I'm having a cup of coffee."

Conor sighed. He kept his voice low as he spoke. "You know what I mean. You're taking her out for a walk, like she's some woman you're dating instead of—."

"Our prisoner?" Declan finished. He glanced over his shoulder at the other people in the room. "Could you excuse us for a minute?"

Walsh, Murphy, and Ezra got up and left the kitchen. Walsh hung back, probably hoping he would overhear something. Declan waited until Walsh walked away before he continued.

Chapter 14

"It's Liv, Conor, not some random woman I barely know. She's a ... friend and someone I've known for eight years."

"No, you *knew* her eight years ago," Conor said. "She's not the same person. You know nothing about this woman. You remember the girl she used to be. Be careful."

Declan sighed. "I've kept her cooped up for more than a week. I'm taking her out to the backyard to get some fresh air. It's not like there's anywhere for her to go." He pulled back his jacket to reveal his gun. "Olivia won't run."

Conor crossed his arms over his chest. "At least let me go out there with you."

Declan snorted. "I'll be fine. If it makes you feel better, hang out on the porch and watch. I'm not worried about Olivia overpowering me and taking off, though."

Conor rolled his eyes. "You're the boss," he muttered. "But you need to remember, Olivia is the daughter of a mobster. She is not innocent. Far from it. She manipulated her bodyguard into helping her get out of her marriage to Clyde. She's a lot more cunning than that innocent face would have you think."

"I'm not easily manipulated, Conor." Declan downed the rest of his coffee and tossed the cup in the sink. "But your opinion is noted."

Olivia stepped into the kitchen. She had put on a too-tight sweater and the sweatpants he had given her. She had wrapped her arms around herself and refused to make eye contact with either of them. As she walked past Conor, she kept her head down. Declan took a jacket off a hook by the door, handed it to Olivia, and ushered her out the back door.

Olivia walked down the porch steps, stopped, and turned to look at Declan, who stood on the porch, watching her.

"Are you coming?" she asked.

Declan nodded. "The best we can do is walk around the backyard."

It was a large backyard with a high fence. No one was in sight, so they could wander around the yard without worry.

They walked in silence around the yard, side by side. Declan couldn't help but wonder how Conor expected Olivia to manipulate him when she didn't even talk to him.

They'd walked around the yard several times when Olivia stopped, tipped her head back, and dragged in a deep breath.

"Thank you," she whispered. "I was going stir crazy locked in that room." She cleared her throat. "I'm guessing your men gave you grief about this, huh?"

Declan chuckled. "What makes you think that?"

Olivia looked over her shoulder. Conor was on the porch, leaning against the railing and attempting to look like he wasn't watching their every move.

"Yeah, they think—well, Conor thinks—you're trying to manipulate me."

Olivia laughed. "Does he know about us? Your feelings for me?"

Declan shook his head. "No, he doesn't."

"Don't think I haven't thought about it," Olivia said. "Manipulating you, I mean."

"Oh, really?"

"It wouldn't do any good, though," Olivia said. "You never appeared to be a man who can be easily influenced. Trust me, I've known both types. There are men who will

Chapter 14

do anything you ask if it means getting you into their bed. Then there are men like you. Strong-willed, determined, and unwilling to let anything or anyone sway them from the path they are on. You have a destination in mind. I doubt you'll change your mind because of a woman in a short skirt." She paused and looked down at herself. "Or maybe I should say, a woman in oversized blue sweatpants."

Declan chuckled and nodded. "You're right. I will not turn from the path I've set myself on. I won't stop. Not until I've reached the end and I've done what I need to do."

Olivia put her hand on his arm and stared up at him. When he looked into her eyes, it transported him to the past. He resisted the sudden urge to pull her into his arms while Conor watched them.

"What do you need to do, Declan?" she asked. "What do you mean when you say you won't stop?"

Declan closed his eyes and sucked in a deep breath.

"I won't stop until Clyde Braniff is dead."

Chapter 15
Olivia

I won't stop until Clyde Braniff is dead.
Declan's words played on repeat in Olivia's head. Eighteen hours later, she was still thinking about them. He planned to kill Clyde.

Olivia didn't know if it was even possible. Could Declan kill Clyde? She knew if, given the opportunity, he would attempt it; the real question was whether Declan could get to Clyde and kill him before Clyde's men intervened. They protected the man better than the president. Maybe better.

If Declan could somehow get to Clyde, she wanted to be there to witness his death. She needed to see it. She hoped to hear Clyde scream and beg for his life. Ultimately, she prayed she would see him bleed. Witnessing his demise would help heal her broken soul.

Olivia vowed to stay alive long enough to see it happen. She would do anything to help destroy Clyde. Anything.

After eating dinner with her, Declan informed her of his plan to send Walsh and Murphy to Ohio. Once they were on the road, he and Conor planned to disappear. Declan wanted her to go with them. When she questioned

Chapter 15

him about his plans to eliminate Clyde, he wouldn't expand on them, only assured her it would happen.

"I am determined to make it happen," he muttered.

Declan kissed the corner of her mouth when he left her, and he didn't lock the door. She could go to the bathroom and clean up, and she even went downstairs to check on Drew. She passed Conor in the hall on the way but didn't say anything; he merely smiled and nodded before stepping into one of the other rooms.

Drew was asleep when she entered his room. She didn't want to wake him up, so she gave him a quick once-over to make sure his bandages were in place and no infections were visible. Then she returned to her room. She intended to stay as far away from Walsh as possible, less chance of him figuring out who she was. If she slipped and he discovered she was Clyde's runaway bride, she knew Walsh would serve her up on a silver platter to the mob boss. Staying away from him was the safest strategy.

Olivia reflected on the last week as she lay on the bed. But the one thing her mind kept returning to was Declan.

The memory of the kiss they'd shared the night before lingered like the scent of roses in a flower shop. She couldn't stop thinking about how warm and solid Declan was, how he tasted like warm whiskey and smelled like leather and gunpowder. His touch was gentle, his caresses gentle. Olivia had forgotten what it was like to be in his arms and now that she had experienced it again, she didn't want it to end. She was falling back in love with Declan Quinn: bank robber, mobster, and kidnapper. Her kidnapper.

After growing up with a mobster for a father, Olivia vowed she would never get involved with a man in the same business. She was done with that life: the terror, the pain, the agony of living life in the Mafia. Getting out of that life was her only goal. Growing up, she'd lived in fear something would happen to her family because of the life her father led. Her father took away her chance to get out when he forced her into an engagement to satisfy family obligations.

She wanted Declan, and she hated herself for it.

Olivia drifted in and out of sleep, the thoughts in her head mingling with the dreams her subconscious created. The sound of the door opening and closing pulled her back to reality. She scrambled out of the bed and squinted into the darkness.

"Hello?" she whispered.

Someone reached for her in the dark, their hand closing around her upper arm and yanking her close. Instinct took over, and she lashed out, her hand landing a blow on the person's chest and her foot connecting with their shin. She let out a startled squeak as she scrambled to get away.

"Hey, hey, it's okay, Liv. It's me, Declan."

His deep, raspy voice was unmistakable. Olivia let out a shaky breath and tried to relax, despite her pounding heart.

"You scared me," she muttered.

"I'm sorry. I didn't mean to frighten you," Declan said. He released her and took a step back.

"I just … for a second, it brought back—," she whispered. "Clyde, uh, he did … things to me." She squeezed her hands together in front of her and prayed they would stop shaking.

Declan rubbed her upper arm. "What did he do to you?" he asked.

Chapter 15

Olivia shook her head. "I-I can't." She hadn't told anyone what Clyde had done to her. Her breath caught in her throat, and she had to swallow an unexpected sob rising from her chest. She turned her back on Declan and put her hand over her mouth. Shame washed over her.

Declan came up behind her, and his huge, warm hands settled on her hips and light stubble scratched her neck as he pressed his mouth to her ear. "I am so sorry he hurt you. I swear to God, I will make him pay for it." He rested his cheek against the side of her head.

"I don't need you to fight my battles for me, Declan," she whispered.

"I know," he replied. "But I want to do it. For both of us." He kissed her temple. "I hate that you're afraid."

Olivia stated confidently, "I'm not afraid of you."

"Liv, I promise I won't hurt you."

Olivia leaned back and rested her head on his shoulder. "I know. I trust you." She put her hands over his, tugging on them until he completely wrapped her in his arms. "Help me not be afraid anymore, Declan. It's been so long since I felt anything good."

"Close your eyes," he whispered. "Trust me." He slid his hands down her hips to the apex of her thighs, then lowered them until his fingers skimmed the top of her underwear.

Olivia took a deep breath and closed her eyes. This was Declan. He wouldn't hurt her. He couldn't.

Declan slipped his fingers into her underwear and between her legs. He found her clit with his middle finger and rubbed it slowly.

Olivia gasped, and her hips jerked toward his hand. She leaned against his chest as he slipped his hand into her underwear, and his long finger entered her.

"There you go, baby," he whispered. "I got you."

He pressed his thumb against her clit, sending an electric jolt rushing through her. If Declan hadn't been holding her waist, she might have fallen. Olivia groaned as he circled the sensitive nub of nerves with his thumb, and his finger pumped in and out of her. His lips found her earlobe, and he sucked it into his mouth as he took a single step toward the bed.

The movement caused Declan's hand to move inside her, sending a shot of pure bliss right through her. Olivia trembled, her knees shaking, and when he did it again, she had to hold back her scream of pleasure. Declan smiled against her neck and took another step forward. He eased a second finger into her entrance, his entire palm pressed against her. They stood at the side of the bed: her body held tight against his chest, his lips on her neck, his fingers moving inside her at a maddening pace.

Declan pushed his hips into her back and urged her to move, rocking Olivia's body against his hand. "Come on, sweetheart," he whispered in her ear. His breath tore in and out of his throat, making his voice impossibly deep and sexy.

Olivia's hips jerked as she ground against Declan's hand, filthy moans helplessly falling from her lips.

"Oh, fuck, baby, that's it," Declan groaned.

Olivia whimpered at the feeling of fullness as a third finger joined the other two, and desire overwhelmed her.

"Let go, Liv. Let me take care of you," he urged.

Olivia grabbed the hand Declan had around her waist and tugged, guiding it to her breast, the nipple hard and erect, pushing against the fabric of the shirt she wore. Declan rolled it between his thumb and forefinger, sending a sharp sensation shooting through her.

Chapter 15

She dug her nails into his arm right above his wrist, and her hips bucked as he fucked her with his fingers. Her body was wound tight, approaching an orgasm, something she hadn't experienced in years. Olivia tensed in anticipation.

Declan's movements slowed, and his lips moved back to her ear. "Relax, Liv. Take a deep breath, and let it happen." He caressed her as he nibbled at her neck, kneading her breast with his other hand.

Olivia took a deep breath and released it. She closed her eyes and leaned back against Declan's chest.

"Yeah, that's my girl," he whispered as he pumped his fingers, twisting them so he brushed against her sweet spot. He slid his other hand down her waist and between her legs, finding her clit with his fingers.

"Right there," Olivia gasped. "Oh my God, right there."

Declan plunged his fingers in and out of her, hitting her sweet spot with each thrust of his fingers. His mouth closed over her pulse point and he sucked, the dual sensations too much for her to take.

She let go in a burst of pure pleasure. Her eyes rolled back in her head, and every nerve ending ignited as she had the most mind-blowing orgasm she had ever experienced. Her brain short-circuited, and she lost awareness of everything but Declan.

He lowered her to the bed, still kissing her neck. Olivia laid on her stomach, her head on her arms, her body trembling from the aftershocks of the intense orgasm she had experienced. Declan laid beside her and brushed her hair from her face. She turned to face him and put her hand on his cheek.

"Thank you," she said. "That was amazing. I forgot how wonderful it could be with someone you—." Her mouth snapped shut. She couldn't bring herself to say the words.

Declan pulled her back into his arms and peppered her face with kisses. "You don't need me in your life, *macushla*. I'm bad news, no good for you. I need to let you go." His arms tightened around her, contradicting the words he had just said.

Olivia shook her head. "No. Don't say that."

Declan sighed. "Olivia—."

She buried her face against his chest and shook her head. She refused to listen to him, refused to entertain the thought that she would lose him before she got him back. There was no turning back for her. She was too far gone. Not now, not after everything. Olivia had damned herself and fallen in love with a mobster.

Chapter 16
Olivia

The crack of a gunshot echoed through the room, dragging Olivia from a deep sleep. She shot upright, a choked scream coming out of her. The blankets wrapped around her legs, trapping and holding her hostage. A heavy weight settled on her waist.

"Don't touch me," she muttered.

"Liv?" A deep, husky voice broke through the wall of sleep. "Liv?" Calloused fingers squeezed her waist under her shirt, and warm breath tickled her earlobe. "It's okay."

Olivia opened her eyes and squinted in the dark room. She couldn't see anything. Declan laid beside her, his hand on her waist.

"Are you okay?" he asked. "What was that?"

"I heard … I heard a gunshot," Olivia stammered.

Declan pulled her into his arms. "It was thunder, not a gunshot. You're safe."

Olivia closed her eyes and took a deep breath. "I'm … I'm okay. Sorry."

Declan kissed the center of her forehead. He dragged his legs out from beneath the blankets to sit on the side of the bed. Rubbing his face and stretching, his muscular arms almost burst the seams of his shirt. He bent over and picked up his shoes.

"Where are you going?" Olivia whispered.

Declan smiled at her over his shoulder. "I'm going to put on some clean clothes and check on Drew," he replied. He dropped his shoes back on the floor, turned to Olivia, and gathered her in his arms. He took her chin in his hand, tilted her head back, and kissed her. It took her breath away. When he was done, he rose to his feet and slipped on his shoes.

"I'll bring you something to eat after I check on my brother," he said.

"I should come with you," Olivia said. "Check his bandages and stitches."

"That would be great," Declan said. "I'll meet you in his room. Do you remember where it is?"

"Downstairs, second door from the stairs. Right?"

Declan nodded. "I'll see you in a few minutes."

Olivia watched Declan as he left the room with his messy hair and wrinkled clothes. If anyone saw him and the state he was in between her room and his, they would know immediately what they had been doing. The thought made her blush.

Once the door closed behind him, she climbed out of the bed and put on the clothes Ezra had given her. She went to the bathroom, washed her face, and brushed her teeth before she headed downstairs to Drew's room.

Declan stood in Drew's room, laughing at something his brother had said. He smiled at Olivia when she entered and gestured for her to join him.

"Hi again," Drew said. "Did you come to make sure I was behaving myself?"

Chapter 16

Olivia laughed. "It looks like you're doing well. Are you eating and drinking?"

Drew nodded in answer to her question.

"Have you walked around at all?" she asked.

"A little, when I had to go to the bathroom." He blushed and stared at the blankets covering his legs.

"That's good," Olivia said. She wanted to ask him if he'd noticed any blood in his urine or anything, but she didn't want to embarrass him anymore than she already had. She recalled that he was shy and quiet, unlike his brother Declan. Maybe that hadn't changed much in the last eight years.

"I'll go see if Ezra cooked up anything for breakfast. I'll be right back." Declan squeezed Olivia's hand and nodded at his brother before he disappeared out the door.

An awkward silence settled in the room after Declan's departure. Olivia perched on the edge of the chair with her hands folded in her lap. Drew cleared his throat.

"Are you sure we don't know each other?" he asked. "I can't get over this feeling that I somehow know you."

Olivia fidgeted. She didn't know if she should tell Drew or not.

"Olivia?" Drew mumbled under his breath. A grin spread across his face. "Liv. You're Liv O'Reilly. I knew I recognized you." The grin faded, and Drew swallowed loudly. "Holy shit. What did my brother do?"

"Drew—."

Drew shook his head. "What did Declan do?"

"I ... He ..." Olivia took a deep breath. She lowered her voice to a whisper before she spoke. "I worked at the last bank he robbed. I saw his face, heard his name. He didn't want me to go to the FBI, so he took me. He didn't know who I was."

"But he does now?" Drew asked.

Olivia gnawed on her lower lip and nodded.

"Clyde will kill him if he finds out you're with Declan. Does my brother know that? Does he understand that?"

"Clyde doesn't know I'm here," Olivia insisted. "He has no idea. And yes, I'm sure Declan is aware of the danger."

Drew pushed himself upright and leaned forward, the intensity of his expression frightening Olivia.

"He will find out," Drew said. "If he hasn't already." He swallowed and grimaced as he sat back against the pillows on the bed. "Not all of Declan's men are loyal."

"Does Declan know that?" Olivia asked.

Drew nodded. "Yeah, he knows. It's just a matter of time before Clyde finds out you're here."

"Only Declan and Conor know who I am. And now you," Olivia said. "Walsh and Murphy don't know."

"You can't be sure of that," Drew said. He grimaced as he shifted uneasily. "Clyde has a way … a way of knowing things. You know that, though, don't you?"

Olivia sighed. "Yes, I do. And you're right. I was cautiously optimistic, and I shouldn't have been. I haven't been as careful as I normally would be."

"You know what Clyde is capable of, don't you?" Drew asked. "You have to know."

"I know," Olivia whispered. She squeezed her hands together in her lap. "I know what he did to Sarah too."

Drew crossed his arms over his chest. "You know what he did? Exactly what he did?"

Olivia shook her head. "N-no," she stammered. "I know he killed her."

"He didn't just kill her." Drew closed his eyes and when he spoke, his voice was so low, Olivia struggled to hear him. "Clyde and his men tortured Sarah for hours. Clyde

Chapter 16

beat her. He … he raped her. He let his men rape her. I could hear her screaming, begging them to stop. When Clyde finished with her and she couldn't take anymore, he killed her. He snapped her neck. His men dragged her into the room I was in and dumped her on the floor in front of me. He made me watch while they shoved her in a wooden box. It was a reminder of what Clyde could and would do if Declan didn't cooperate. Then he had his men deliver her to Declan. Clyde laughed when he told me they left the box in the middle of the living room for Declan to find. He *laughed*. Like it was the funniest thing ever. Clyde told me if Declan didn't cooperate, I would be next. They backed Declan into a corner. His grief and anger over what happened to Sarah drove him to finish what Clyde made him start. He felt like he had no choice."

"I overheard Declan tell Clyde it's been more than a year," Olivia whispered. "How much longer does Clyde expect Declan to do this?"

Drew shrugged. "Clyde's greedy. No amount of money or power will ever be enough. He has an endgame, but no one knows what it is. And he knew as long as he had me, Declan would do whatever he wanted. My brother didn't want to lose anyone else."

"Why did he kill Sarah instead of you?" Olivia asked.

"Clyde flipped a coin," Drew said. "He took a goddamn coin out of his pocket and flipped it. Heads, I was dead; tails, it was Sarah. It was tails."

"What the fuck did you just say?" Declan stood in the doorway, shocked. The dishes on the tray in his hands shook as he trembled.

"Declan, I'm so sorry," Drew said. "I was going to tell you—"

"That fucking asshole decided who lived and who died by flipping a coin?" Declan stepped into the room and dropped the tray of food on the end of the bed. "I'm not just going to kill him; I am going to make him fucking suffer. He will *beg* me to kill him."

Declan spun around and stumbled out the door. Olivia heard him running down the stairs and then, a minute later, the sound of a door slamming echoed through the house. She got to her feet and moved to the door. It was as if she was walking through a dense fog. She stopped with her hand on the door handle, absentmindedly twisting it back and forth. She contemplated whether she should go after him or wait.

"Go," Drew said. "He needs someone."

Olivia looked at Drew over her shoulder. He nodded at her. Decision made, she threw open the door and went down the hall. She didn't know what she was going to say or do, but that didn't matter. All that mattered was Declan needed her.

Chapter 17
Declan

Declan burst through the back door onto the porch wrapped around the rear of the house. He stumbled down the steps into the rain, a desperate attempt to get away from Drew's words and to quell the images running through his head. He stopped under the gigantic oak tree in a far corner of the yard.

The flip of a coin.

The flip of a coin had decided the murder of his sister, a beautiful young woman with a promising future. Declan slid to the wet ground, his head in his hands. He hadn't known. The details of Sarah's death were not something he'd been privy to; Clyde's only concern was Declan understanding his sister was dead and the same could happen to his brother. Clyde hadn't shared the details.

He rested his head against the tree and closed his eyes as he fought to control his emotions. The memory of that night consumed him.

Declan slammed the back door hard enough to make the glass in the kitchen window rattle. He stripped off his coat, threw it on the back of the nearest kitchen chair, grabbed an unopened bottle of whiskey and a glass from the cupboard, and filled it halfway. He leaned against the counter, stared at the floor, and waited for the phone to ring.

Clyde would call; Declan knew it. It wasn't everyday he refused to do the bidding of a notorious mobster. Clyde would have something to say about it. Declan couldn't believe he hadn't heard from the soon-to-be head of the Muldoon family already. He took a drink from the glass in his hand and made his way through the dark house to the living room. He reached for the light on a low table by the front door. That was when he noticed it.

A rectangular box, three feet long and two feet wide, sat in the middle of the room, the sofa and coffee table shoved out of the way to make room for it. It wasn't anything special, just a plain wooden box, devoid of any markings of any kind. It was nailed shut.

Declan stared at the box and took a step closer. He waited, though he didn't know what for. He set his drink on the table beside the lamp with a shaking hand. Whiskey sloshed over the side of the glass and onto the floor. It would piss Sarah off when she saw it.

Declan pivoted, hurried back to the kitchen, and grabbed a screwdriver and hammer from the cabinet under the sink. Next to the box, he dropped to his knees, inserted the screwdriver under the lid's edge, and then dislodged the nail with the hammer. He did it again and again until he tore every nail loose. He dropped the screwdriver and hammer on the floor, took a staggering breath, and pushed the lid off the box.

Sarah's lifeless body was inside, one arm twisted awkwardly behind her, her knees bent and resting against her chest. Her neck was at an odd angle, and her long hair

Chapter 17

covered her face. Every inch of visible skin was covered with bruises, and someone ripped and tore her clothes.

"No, no, no, no, no," Declan muttered under his breath. He reached into the box, slid his arms under his sister's body, and pulled her free. She was limp and cold to the touch.

"Sarah? Can you hear me?" he whispered. He pushed her hair out of her face, grimacing at the tacky feel of blood on his hands.

Her hazel eyes were glazed over, lifeless, and her head drooped to one side. A guttural moan escaped Declan, as he pulled her closer and pressed his head to her chest.

"Please, Sarah, please," he whispered under his breath, praying to a God he no longer believed in that his little sister was still alive.

Sarah was dead. Clyde had given Declan his answer.

Declan shook his head and pulled himself from the cursed memory he fought so hard to keep at bay. Every day, he struggled to keep his emotions in check and to keep himself from losing control.

He had found the note in her hand, covered in her blood.

I made your sister mine in every sense of the word. She screamed your name as she died, begging for you to come and save her. Give me one year, or this will be your brother.

Clyde left him no choice but to do as he asked. If Declan refused, the only family he had left in the world would face the same fate as Sarah. It was something he couldn't let happen. He did the only thing he could do; he went to work for the Mafia boss who murdered his sister.

Now Drew was free and safe, but Declan wanted Clyde dead now more than ever. He had to pay for what he'd done. Not only for what he'd done to Sarah, but for what Declan suspected Clyde had done to Olivia. If Declan had any chance of keeping Olivia safe, Clyde could not stay alive.

They needed to leave soon. He would get Walsh and Murphy on the road to Ohio, get them out of his way, then he would take Drew and Olivia and go someplace safe. Only then could he figure out how to get to Clyde.

A crack of thunder exploded in the air, and the cloudy sky turned black. The rain came down harder, a deluge, making it difficult to see more than two or three feet in front of himself. The rain soaked through his clothes.

"Declan!" Olivia called.

He squinted, trying to see through the pouring rain. Olivia stepped off the back of the porch and ran toward him. He held his arms out, and she threw herself into them. She buried her face against the side of his neck.

"What are you doing out here?" Declan asked. "You're getting soaked."

"So are you," she said. "Come inside with me. Please?"

Declan pressed a kiss to Olivia's forehead. "I need you to listen to me, Liv. I have to leave for a little while. There are some things I need to handle. I'll be gone for a couple of hours, then when I get back, we'll go. We'll find someplace safe until I can take care of Clyde."

Olivia shook her head. "No, Declan. I think you need to let it go. We can walk away and never look back. I'll tell you where the money is. We can go get it, and we can disappear." She looked up at him as the rain fell on her face. "Forget about Clyde. Forget about Boston. It's time to forget the past that haunts us. We can just go."

Chapter 17

"No. I have to do this. If I don't, you will never be safe. Drew will never be safe." He kissed her, desperate to claim her, to keep her close, to make her understand what he needed to do. "Please try to understand. I *have* to do this. I told you before that I won't stop until Clyde is dead."

Olivia sighed, but she nodded. She stepped out of his arms and wrapped her own around herself. A shiver worked its way through her. "Damn it," she whispered. "I know. I understand, even though I hate it. Clyde has been chasing me for three years. He won't stop. The only way to stop him is to kill him."

Declan put his arm around her shoulder and led her back to the house. "Let's go inside. I need to talk to Conor and get Walsh out of the house." He kissed her temple. "I'll take care of everything."

"What do you mean you're not going with us?" Walsh yelled.

"Calm down, Walsh. I want you and Murph to go to Ohio," Declan explained. "Conor and I will meet you in two days."

"We don't separate. Those are the rules," Walsh said.

"Rules?" Declan said. "What do you mean 'rules'?"

"Clyde's rules." Walsh crossed his arms over his chest and leaned against the wall. "He won't be happy if he finds out we split up."

"It's only for two days, Walsh. Two days. Conor and I will meet you in Mayfield Heights on Friday," Declan said.

"What about the woman?" Murphy interjected.

Declan took a deep breath. "She won't be with us. I'm going to take care of it."

"Are you going to kill her?" Walsh asked.

It was the question he had hoped neither of them would ask, but he knew they would. He had to lie his ass off, convince them he was going to kill Olivia. It wouldn't be easy.

Declan took a deep breath before he spoke. "Yes."

"Bullshit," Walsh snapped. "You've got it bad for that bitch. You won't kill her."

"She will be dead by morning," Declan said.

Walsh snorted. "I doubt it."

Declan was across the room in a split second. He grabbed Walsh by the front of his shirt and slammed him against the wall. "Enough. I don't want to hear another fucking word out of your mouth. Get your shit, and get on the road. You have ten minutes."

He slammed Walsh against the wall one more time for emphasis, then he released him and turned his back on him. He heard the door behind him open and Walsh stomping down the hall. Murphy followed.

Conor cleared his throat. "The second he walks out the front door, Walsh is going to go straight to Clyde."

"I know," Declan said. "I'm hoping by the time Clyde gets here, we'll be long gone."

"Where are we going?" Conor asked. "We can't go back to Boston."

"No. We're going north to New Hampshire."

Conor's eyes widened. "Shane's? Are we going to Shane's?"

Declan nodded. "I haven't asked him yet, but I'm sure he'll say yes. We'll go to Piran's and figure out how to deal with Clyde there."

Declan and Shane Kelly had crossed paths five years ago, shortly before Declan tried to get out. They'd hit it off, to everyone's surprise, especially Shane's. He didn't

Chapter 17

make friends easily. Shane wasn't a guy anyone wanted to mess with; he had no loyalty to either the Muldoons or the O'Reillys. He sold his services to the highest bidder. Shane's loyalty was unwavering and dependable if he considered someone a friend.

When Declan ended Clyde's life, he knew the only person he could trust to help him was Shane Kelly. Now that Drew was free, he could go to Shane and ask for his help.

It was time to end this, once and for all.

Chapter 18
Olivia

Declan had been gone for a little over an hour. Olivia was worried about him, especially after overhearing his conversation with Conor. After Walsh stormed off, Olivia stepped out of the shadows at the end of the hall and headed for Drew's room. She stopped outside the door and heard them talking about Conor's concern that Walsh would go straight to Clyde. The thought of Walsh talking to Clyde terrified her. Declan was gone before she could talk to him about it.

Since Olivia's clothes were soaked from the rainstorm, Ezra gave her a change of clothes. She took a shower to help her warm up, put on the clean clothes, and then went to check on Drew. They talked for a few minutes, but he was tired and wanted to rest, so Olivia wandered downstairs.

Olivia found Ezra in the same room where she'd helped Drew. She peered into the room and saw Ezra sitting on the couch with a ball of yarn and two large knitting needles. She stared out the window at the falling rain.

"Ezra?" Olivia said.

The older woman turned to look at Olivia. "Come in, Ms. O'Reilly."

Chapter 18

Olivia gave her a tentative smile. "You know who I am."

"I'm very familiar with the Muldoons and the O'Reillys," Ezra explained. "The minute I laid eyes on you, I knew you were Sean's daughter."

Olivia stepped into the room and perched on the edge of the nearest chair. "How?"

"I worked at Folger's Café for years. Every mobster that walked through the door was someone I knew. I knew their families too." She worked the needles in her hands, creating something out of nothing as she spoke. "When someone shot up Folger's a few years ago, I sustained injuries. I wanted out, so I packed up my things and moved up here. Now and then I help those boys who were close to my heart."

"Like Declan?" Olivia said.

"Yes, like Declan. I have a soft spot for that one." Ezra smiled and tugged on the yarn in her lap. "I think you do too."

Olivia laughed. "I do." She crossed and uncrossed her ankles and shifted in the chair. "We dated when we were younger."

Ezra looked at her over the top of her glasses. "I remember. I seem to remember you breaking his heart, too."

The laughter died in Olivia's throat. Was that true? Did she break Declan's heart? She knew how hard it was on her when her father forced her to stop seeing Declan; had it been just as difficult for him?

"I never meant to break his heart," she whispered. "But my father—."

"I know, sweetheart," Ezra said. "Your father was a ... demanding man."

Olivia chuckled. "That's an understatement." She sat back in the chair and folded her hands in her lap. "Do you mind if I stay down here? It's lonely upstairs."

Ezra nodded. "If you'd like."

They sat and chatted about mundane things, like the horrible rainstorm outside and the books they'd recently read. Ezra enjoyed talking, and Olivia was content to listen. Once they'd exhausted all topics of conversation, Ezra turned on the TV and they watched it in comfortable silence. Ezra's sudden change of attitude surprised her, but she appreciated it.

"He'll be back soon," Ezra said with a laugh after the ninth or tenth time Olivia checked the time on the grandfather clock in the corner. "Trust me when I say Declan knows what he's doing."

"I know he does," Olivia said. She stood up and stretched. "I'm going to make a cup of tea. Would you like some?"

Ezra shook her head. "No, thank you." She returned to her knitting.

While Olivia waited for the water to boil, she sat at the kitchen table, laid her head down, and closed her eyes. The rain still fell outside, the sound soothing. Her thoughts turned to Declan and all that had happened in the short time she had been with him. The turns her life had taken astounded her, but none more than the one where she fell in love with the mobster who kidnapped her and held her hostage. But there it was, right in front of her, and she couldn't deny it, nor did she want to. She was head over heels for Declan Quinn—again—and there was no turning back.

Returning to her life in Boston had seemed like a pipe dream. She always figured if she returned to Boston, it

Chapter 18

would be to live a life of misery as Clyde Braniff's reluctant wife. She'd resigned herself to a life away from her sister and her parents. Now there was a possibility that she might go home and see them.

For three years, Olivia had lived in fear, so it was hard to even hope that things might improve. Being with Declan, knowing he wanted to protect her and keep her safe, gave her hope.

A crash and a muffled cry from the middle of the house startled her and pulled her from her musings. She sat up and looked toward the swinging kitchen door. Maybe it had been the TV.

"Ezra?" she called. She waited a few seconds, then called her name again. "Ezra?"

There was no answer.

Olivia got out of her seat, instinct telling her to be quiet, and crossed the kitchen. She stopped on her side of the swinging door, pressed her ear against it, and listened. When she didn't hear anything, she pushed open the door, slipped into the hallway, and took several steps toward the library.

"Ezra? Are you all right?" Olivia called again. Still no answer.

She was halfway down the hall, almost to the library, when the scream of the teapot on the stove erupted. Startled, Olivia squeaked, spun on her heel, and hurried back down the hall. She shoved open the kitchen door, ran to the stove, and pulled the kettle off the burner.

Maybe Ezra was upstairs or in the bathroom. Olivia was on edge after everything that had happened and all she had been through. She was jumping at shadows.

The hit came from behind, hard enough to shove her into the stove. The kettle toppled over, hot water leaking from the spot and splashing onto her bare feet. She screamed as her legs gave out and she fell, hitting the wooden floor. Her chin hit so hard, her teeth slammed together, and she bit her tongue, the coppery taste of blood filling her mouth. Olivia tried to push herself to her hands and knees, but before she could, a hand fisted her hair and yanked her head back.

Walsh leered at her. He pulled her to her feet, using her hair, ignoring her whimper of pain. The grin on his face made her blood run cold.

"Hi there, *Liv*," Walsh said. "I know someone who is eager to see you."

Olivia moaned. She closed her eyes and, in a split second, made a decision. She grabbed Walsh's wrist with both hands, holding it tight as she brought her knee up and hit Walsh in the groin.

Walsh went down with a loud grunt, his hand falling out of Olivia's hair as he dropped to one knee. She pushed him backward, stepped over him, and sprinted for the door. Her hip hit the edge of the kitchen table, sending the mugs to the floor with a crash of broken glass. She ran into the swinging door with both hands out and sprinted down the hall, not looking back. She darted into the library. Ezra was sprawled on the floor, facedown, blood pooling under her head. Olivia couldn't tell if she was alive or dead, but she didn't have time to check. She needed a weapon, and she needed it now.

Olivia spun in a circle, looking around the room. On the floor, next to Ezra, was the only thing she could think of using. She snatched up one of the knitting needles and spun around. Walsh stood in the doorway.

"You fucking bitch," he growled. He charged.

Chapter 18

Olivia swung the knitting needle at him, praying she could jam it into his eye or maybe his ear. Instead, she embedded it deep in his upper arm. Blood poured down his arm, staining his white shirt. Walsh screamed, a horrifying, guttural sound that made Olivia's skin crawl.

Walsh pressed a hand to his arm and when he saw the blood on his fingers, another growl left him. He lunged, grabbed Olivia's upper arm, drew back his fist, and punched her in the jaw. She stumbled back and went down, her head hitting the edge of the table by the couch. Black spots filled her vision, and then everything faded away.

Chapter 19
Declan

Conor pulled into the small driveway at the back of the house. The rain had stopped an hour ago while they were gone. The sun was out, and it glistened on the droplets of rain sprinkled across the grass.

Declan climbed out of the car. He pulled his hat down low on his head and hurried up the driveway through the back gate. He didn't want to chance anyone seeing him. Conor stayed close behind him.

Declan was halfway across the yard when he noticed the back door stood wide open. He stopped and looked over every inch of the back of the house, searching for anything that might be out of place. He broke into a run, sprinting across the grass and up the porch steps. As he entered the kitchen, he drew his gun from its holster.

Someone knocked over the tea kettle, and water leaked onto the stove and formed a puddle beneath it. Several mugs were broken on the floor. Declan cleared the kitchen, then he slowly pushed open the swinging kitchen door and eased into the hall. The hallway was empty. He eased down the hall to the library.

Drew was in the library, sitting on the floor with Ezra's head in his lap. She had blood caked in her hair and dripping down the side of her face. Declan had never seen her so pale.

"Jesus Christ, Deck, thank God you're here," Drew said. "They hurt Ezra pretty bad. I think she needs an ambulance."

Declan dropped to a knee beside her and pressed two fingers to the side of her throat. Her pulse was faint, but at least she was alive.

"Ezra?" he whispered. "Ezra, can you hear me?"

"Declan?" Conor yelled from the back of the house.

"I'm in the library," Declan called over his shoulder. A few seconds later, Conor appeared in the doorway.

"Oh, shit. Is she alive?" Conor asked.

Declan nodded. "Barely." He turned to his brother. "Where's Liv?"

"I don't know," Drew muttered. "I was in the shower. When I got out, I felt that something was not right. I came downstairs and found Ezra like this. I called Liv's name, but—."

"She's not here," Declan finished. "Fuck."

Ezra moaned, and her eyelids fluttered.

Declan leaned over her. "Ezra, can you tell me what happened?"

"Walsh," she mumbled.

"Walsh? Did Walsh do this to you?"

Ezra tried to nod, but it must have hurt because as soon as she moved her head, she let out a long, loud moan. She sucked in a shaky breath. "He was here. Hit me and knocked me out." She pressed a hand to her head and winced. "Why … why is my head wet?"

"We're gonna get you some help, okay?" He clutched her hand and leaned over her. "Ezra, where's Olivia? Is she still here?"

"I ... I don't know," Ezra mumbled.

"Hold on, doll," Declan said. He scooped Ezra up and put her on the same couch where an injured Drew had been. Drew took a blanket from the basket on the floor and threw it over her.

Conor crouched next to Ezra. "Walsh did this?" he said. "That dirty bastard. I'm going to kill him."

"Not if I get to him first," Declan growled. "I think he's got Liv."

"It's been less than an hour, Deck," Drew said. "They don't have much of a head start."

"Conor, grab one of those rags from the bar over there and put some water on it. We need to clean Ezra up," Declan ordered. "I think she's got a head wound, not too serious, but I need to get a look under the blood."

Conor did as he was told, then he helped Declan clean Ezra's face and head. Declan was examining her wound when they heard the knock on the door.

It was loud, so loud it echoed through the entire house. Declan gestured to Drew to stay put as he and Conor drew their guns. They stepped into the hall and crept toward the front door. Declan stepped to one side of the door and pulled the curtain on the window open an inch with the tip of his finger. He snarled, yanked open the door, and stuck his gun in the man's face standing in front of him.

"Now, Declan, is that any way to say hello?" Clyde said calmly.

"Where is she, Clyde?" Declan demanded. "Where the *fuck* is she?" He prayed the mob boss wouldn't see how his hand shook as he held the gun inches from his face.

"We should talk," Clyde said. He used two fingers to push the gun aside. "We've got a few things we need

Chapter 19

to discuss." He stepped inside and closed the door behind him.

"We don't have anything to discuss," Declan snapped. "I'm done talking to you about anything. Where the fuck is Olivia?"

Clyde laughed. "My wayward fiancée? She's fine. A little banged-up, but she'll live."

"She better," Declan said. He cocked his gun. "Get out your phone, and call whoever the hell has her and tell them to let her go."

"No, I don't think so. I'm going to hold on to her for a while. I think she could prove useful." Clyde crossed his arms across his chest and leaned against the banister.

"What do you mean, useful?" Declan asked.

"Leverage, my dear boy. Ms. O'Reilly is useful to me because she is leverage." Clyde brushed imaginary dust from the lapel of his jacket.

Declan's stomach twisted. He held back the rage threatening to explode out of him. "Leverage?" It came out as a whisper.

"I have a job for you."

Declan snarled. "I am done working for you."

"One job, Declan. You do this for me, and I will release you from any further obligation. You, your brother, and Ms. O'Reilly can walk away and not look back."

"I told you I am done working for you," Declan muttered.

Clyde shrugged. "If you want to see Liv alive again, you have no choice."

Declan clenched his fists. "What did you say?"

"I will let Olivia O'Reilly live if you do this job for me," Clyde explained. "If you choose not to do as I ask, she is dead."

"Wait a minute," Conor interrupted. "You would kill your fiancée to prove a point? You would kill her to get Declan to do what you want? How fucked up is that?"

Clyde grimaced. "That bitch doesn't mean anything to me. Donovan *ordered* me to marry her. Uncle Donovan insisted; it was supposed to unite the families." Clyde rolled his eyes. "After what she did to me, I couldn't care less about her. She betrayed me, *stole* from me. No one crosses the Muldoons and lives. No one crosses me and lives through it. But I will let Olivia live if you do this job. Your choice, Declan."

"You bastard." Declan dropped his gun on a small table by the door and lunged at Clyde. He knocked him to the floor, put his hands around Clyde's throat, and pressed his thumbs to his windpipe. There was no way he would let Clyde kill another woman that he loved. No fucking way.

"Declan!" Conor yelled. He jumped on his friend's back and struggled to pull him off the smaller man. "Let him go!"

Declan didn't let go, couldn't let go. God, this felt good. He wanted to kill Clyde, choke the life right out of him, except his brother's voice broke through the fog in his brain.

"Declan, stop," Drew said calmly. "If you don't, you won't save Olivia." His younger brother's hand fell on Declan's shoulder, and he leaned over him. "Let him go, Deck. We'll do what he asks. It will save her life."

Declan released Clyde and fell backward, taking Conor with him. Clyde coughed and sputtered as the air rushed back into his lungs, his face beet red. Conor jumped up, grabbed Clyde, and dragged him to his feet. He forced the mob boss down the hall to the dining room.

Chapter 19

Declan climbed to his feet and stared at his brother. "He'll never let us go. He'll kill us, and then he'll kill Liv. We can't trust him."

Drew glanced down the hall, then he lowered his voice. "I know, Deck," he whispered. "But we have to try. We can't let her end up like Sarah."

Declan groaned. If he didn't do what Clyde wanted, that was exactly what would happen. Clyde would kill Olivia and take her away from him. He couldn't let that happen. He had just gotten her back.

"You're right," Declan muttered. "Goddamn it!" He sighed and rubbed the back of his neck. "Let's find out what the little worm wants."

Clyde folded his hands on the table in front of him. "In three days, Sean O'Reilly is moving a large shipment of money and drugs out of Boston, south to Providence. I want that shipment."

Conor laughed. "You want us to steal a shipment of drugs and money from the O'Reilly family? You're joking, right?"

Clyde made a face and cleared his throat. "I don't joke, Conor."

"Then you've lost your mind," Declan interjected.

"No, I haven't," Clyde said. "I know the route, the time, and the day, even the number of men who will be involved in moving it. I know everything. Every piece of information I have, I'll give to you. You will do the rest."

"I don't understand," Declan said. "You are the heir apparent in the Muldoon family. Why risk all-out war between the Muldoons and O'Reillys by stealing a shipment from the O'Reilly family?"

Clyde scrubbed a hand over his face. "I want my uncle out of the picture. For good."

Declan rested his hands on the table and took a deep breath. "You want Donovan Muldoon gone?"

Clyde nodded. "Yes. I am sick of being under my uncle's thumb. Donovan Muldoon will never die. That asshole is going to live fucking forever. And as long as he's alive, I will be forever beholden to him. He constantly reminds me it's his money, his men, his home, all of it is his. I need something that is mine. *Mine*." He slammed his fists on the table. "I'm sick of begging my uncle for everything I need. This is my way of taking control."

Conor snorted. "That's what all of this has been about? You don't want to ask your uncle to pay for your coffee anymore?"

"Fuck you, Sullivan." Clyde clenched his fists and took a deep breath. "Declan? What's it going to be? Is Olivia going to live or die?"

Declan closed his eyes. If he killed Clyde, he would never find Olivia. But he wasn't sure he could trust the mobster.

"I've heard this shit before," Declan said. "Then you killed my little sister and held my brother hostage for a year. Forgive me if I don't trust you."

Clyde shrugged. "I understand, Declan, I do. All I can do is promise you that this will be the last time. You'll have to take my word for it."

Declan had no choice. He had to save Olivia.

"Okay," Declan whispered. "I'll do it."

Clyde rose to his feet, a victorious smile on his face. "I expect you to be in Boston by tomorrow night. I'll be

Chapter 19

waiting." He straightened the cuffs beneath the sleeves of his jacket as he stepped away from the table. He stopped in the doorway to look back at the three men sitting at the dining room table. "I'll see you in Boston, boys."

The dining room was silent, even after the front door closed behind Clyde. Conor jumped to his feet and paced the room, muttering under his breath.

Declan turned to his brother. "Do you know anything about this job, Drew? Anything at all?"

"You hear a lot when no one thinks you're listening," Drew said. "Clyde has been talking about this job for weeks. He has a man inside, working with the O'Reillys. That's why he knows everything about this shipment. Donovan Muldoon does not know what Clyde has planned."

"Do you know the man inside?" Conor asked.

Drew shook his head. "No. Clyde was careful never to mention his name. I don't think anybody but Clyde knows who it is."

"He wants us in Boston," Conor interjected. "That means he's taking Olivia to Boston. He'll want her close."

"The Muldoon compound is a goddamn fortress," Drew said.

"You got out," Conor said.

Drew shook his head. "I did. Thanks to Ruth. We're going to need her help."

"She'll get us in," Declan said. "And we'll get Olivia out. We're going to Boston. But we're not going to steal O'Reilly's shipment. We're going to get Liv out. I'm getting her back. Then I'm taking Clyde down, once and for all."

Chapter 20
Olivia

Olivia woke up gradually. The sounds registered first: faint music coming from somewhere, the thump of tires on the pavement, the sound of other vehicles nearby. She opened her eyes, but she couldn't see anything. It was too dark, no light visible at all. She tried to sit up, but she met resistance, something hard and metal inches from her face.

It came back to her in bits and pieces—a screaming tea kettle, a knitting needle, blood, Walsh, falling, then nothing.

Her head hurt. She found a lump on her temple above her left ear. Her fingers came away sticky and even though she couldn't see it, she suspected it was blood. Hot tears burned her eyes. She held them back by sheer force of will.

Olivia took a deep breath, and the smell of exhaust filled her nostrils, gagging and choking her. She coughed, which made her head hurt even more. She realized she was in the trunk of a car, hurtling toward an unknown destination.

The darkness prevented her from seeing the time on her watch. It was unclear how long she was in the trunk of

Chapter 20

this car, ranging from minutes to hours. She didn't know. Everything was a blur.

The car slowed, turned a corner, then sped up again. A few minutes later, it slowed again; she heard voices, and the sound of a gate rattling open.

Olivia closed her eyes and pinched the bridge of her nose. There was only one place they could be.

The Muldoon compound.

The car stopped, and the engine cut out. She expected someone to let her out immediately, but it seemed like forever before the trunk opened. Fresh air rushed in, and bright lights assaulted her. Olivia shielded her eyes with one hand and tried to sit up.

Staring down at her was that bastard Walsh. A blood-soaked bandage covered his arm where she'd stabbed him with the knitting needle. He grabbed her upper arm, dragged her roughly from the trunk, and set her on her bare feet on ice-cold asphalt. Olivia shivered.

"Let's go." Walsh held her arm and led her up a short set of stairs and inside the Muldoon mansion.

They stopped in the large foyer, right in front of Clyde Braniff. Olivia's mouth went dry, and she thought she might faint.

"Olivia, how good of you to return home." Clyde smiled, though it didn't reach his eyes. "Take her upstairs. Ruth is waiting. She'll take Olivia to her room."

"What do you want, Clyde?" Olivia asked.

"You know damn well what I want," the mobster snapped. "Lucky for you, I have a meeting in downtown Boston, so we will have to discuss it later." He jerked his chin toward the stairs. "Take her upstairs."

Walsh gripped her arm tight and dragged her up the large stairs to the second floor. A gorgeous, petite woman with long, dark brown hair waited at the top. She smiled at Olivia.

"Hello, love. My name is Ruth." She turned to Walsh. "Thank you, dear. I'll take it from here." Her Scottish accent was thick and lilting. She wiggled her fingers at him. "You can go."

Walsh narrowed his eyes but did as he was told. Ruth pointed down the long, dimly lit hallway. "This way, please."

Olivia knew where they were going; the Muldoon compound was huge, but she had lived there long enough to know the layout of the house. Ruth was taking her to her old room.

Sure enough, they stopped outside a closed door. Ruth opened the door, put her hand in the middle of Olivia's back, and ushered her inside.

"Are you okay, dearie?" Ruth asked, as she closed the door.

Olivia shook her head. "No. My head hurts. I'm dizzy and nauseous. I most likely have a concussion."

Ruth gave her an odd look.

"I was, uh, a nurse. In a former life." She pushed a hand through her hair, crossed the room, and sat on the bed. "I also stink of grease, gasoline, and sweat. I could use a shower."

Ruth pointed to a closed door. "Bathroom is over there."

Olivia nodded. "I know. This was, uh, my room, a long time ago. Three years ago." She cleared her throat and rubbed her forehead. "I'm back where I started."

Olivia hated this room: it was huge, opulent, and ostentatious. An enormous four-poster bed dominated one end of the room, covered in decadent linens and silk throw pillows. The room was full of furniture, crowded with too much in her opinion, despite the size of the

Chapter 20

room. They set up the center of the room as a seating area with a chaise lounge, two chairs, and a table. Next to the door was a sofa, an ottoman, and two more chairs. A fire roared in the fireplace on one side of the room, the logs snapping and crackling, heat pouring from it. Just being back here made her want to crawl out of her skin.

Ruth cleared her throat. "You go take a shower. I'll make you some tea."

Olivia sat on the edge of the bed until Ruth left, closing and locking the door behind her. She rose to her feet, wobbling unsteadily, her head aching with every step. It was like someone was using her head as a bass drum. She held onto the edge of the bed for a second before she crossed the room and opened the top drawer of the dresser.

Inside were her bras, underwear, and socks, things she left behind when she escaped the compound. She slammed the drawer and opened the one below it. More of her clothes.

"Dammit," she muttered. She yanked clean clothes out of the drawer and went into the bathroom.

Brand new toiletries were on the bathroom counter. It was like she'd never left.

Olivia stopped in front of the mirror. A line of dried blood ran from her temple, down her cheek to her chin. She had a large lump an inch above her temple, purple and tender to the touch. She tipped her head back and gazed at her chin in the mirror, noting the bruise that had bloomed on the lower half of her face.

Olivia hated to use anything that Clyde Braniff left for her, but she couldn't stand another minute smelling like the trunk of a car. She rushed through her shower and got dressed. While she was braiding her hair, the door opened, and Ruth entered with a tray. She set it on a low table between two chairs in the center of the room.

"I brought you tea, food, and some aspirin. You should get some rest. If you need anything, knock on the door, and the boys will get me." Ruth turned to leave.

"Wait."

Ruth stopped with her hand on the doorknob. She looked back over her shoulder. "Yes, dearie?"

"What's going to happen to me?" Olivia asked.

"Well, I think that depends on Declan, don't you?" She winked, opened the door, and left.

As the door closed behind Ruth, Olivia glimpsed two men outside. She didn't recognize either of them. The taller of the two turned to look at her, giving her a suggestive, lewd grin as the door swung closed.

Olivia couldn't sleep. She wished she could because when she slept, she dreamed. Her dreams were about Declan touching her, kissing her, holding her, making her feel everything she forgot she could feel. But sleep wouldn't come.

Instead, she lay in the dark room, staring at the ceiling. The only light came from the embers in the fireplace. Men guarded her room constantly, rotating every few hours, and they had locked every door and window in the room.

Every time the door opened, she expected to see Clyde. When she lived in the Muldoon compound three years earlier, visits from Clyde had been a nightly experience. The first time he had come to her room, she thought they could talk, get to know each other. She had been so wrong.

Chapter 20

Clyde stepped into the room, closed the door, and leaned against it. He reached back and locked the door. His smile seemed friendly.

"Hello, Olivia," he crooned.

She gave him an uneasy half-smile. "Hi," she whispered.

Clyde took a step closer. "I thought we could spend some time getting to know each other."

Olivia nodded. "I think that's a great idea."

Clyde stalked across the room. He took hold of her wrist, dragged her from the chair she was sitting in to her feet, and yanked her close. His mouth closed over hers, his tongue stabbing at her tight lips. His arm snaked around her waist, slid up her back, and into her hair. He tangled his fingers in it and tugged, pulling it so hard she let out a startled squeak.

He narrowed his eyes and stared at her. "Open your mouth, Olivia."

She shook her head. "What the hell do you think you're doing?"

Clyde rolled his eyes. "This isn't some sweet, get-to-know-each-other-before-we-get-married moment, Ms. O'Reilly. I honestly have no interest in a relationship with you. As far as I'm concerned, you are a tool to get me what I want. My uncle's money. Which I can't have without an heir. You will give me an heir. And maybe some fun while we're at it."

"That doesn't sound fun to me." Olivia tried to pull away, but Clyde tightened his grip on her. "Let me go."

"No." He shoved her backward onto the bed and descended on her.

Before she knew what was happening, Clyde had ripped her clothes from her body. When she tried to crawl away, he grabbed her by the ankle, yanked her back down onto the bed, and backhanded her. He pressed his arm to her windpipe and leaned over her.

"Do not fight me or you will regret it." He held her in place as he reached down and unbuttoned his pants.

Olivia closed her eyes and tried to imagine she was anywhere but in the Muldoon compound. Tears poured down her face as Clyde assaulted her.

When it was over, he straightened his clothes and left her lying on the bed, sobbing.

"Ms. O'Reilly? Are you alright, dearie?"

Olivia jumped up from the sofa. She hadn't realized Ruth had come into the room. She nodded, wiped away the tears at the corner of her eyes, and cleared her throat. "I'm fine."

"I brought you some brandy," Ruth said. She set a glass decanter on the small table, along with two glasses, then she sat down and filled the glasses.

Ruth surprised Olivia by staying. She sat down across from her, picked up the glass of brandy, and rested her head against the back of the couch.

"Why are you here, Ruth?" she asked. "Why do you work for a man like Clyde?"

Ruth stared at a spot above Olivia's head while she spoke, either refusing to or unable to make eye contact. "Well, some people, like your Declan, do it because Clyde gives them no choice." She tipped her head toward the door. "Others, like Walsh out there, do it for the money

Chapter 20

or some kind of inexplicable power. Then there's me. I work for the Muldoons because I want to."

Olivia cringed and involuntarily flinched at the thought of working for a man like Clyde or Donovan because one *wanted* to. She couldn't imagine it. She was a little afraid of Ruth after her revelation.

Ruth must have noticed Olivia's reaction because she gave the other woman a tight smile and shook her head. "It's not what you think." She glanced over her shoulder at the closed door, got to her feet, and moved to sit on the couch beside Olivia. Ruth patted her on the leg. When she spoke, she kept her voice low.

"Donovan Muldoon killed my father."

Olivia grabbed Ruth's hand. "What?"

Ruth nodded. "My father came to the United States years ago when I was just a child. My mother and I stayed in Scotland while my father came here to work. We planned to join him when he was settled. Six months after he arrived, my mother received a phone call from the States telling us my father was dead."

"It was Muldoon?" Olivia asked.

"And his men," Ruth said. She stared at the floor as she spoke. "My father witnessed a murder. He went to the police. A dirty cop told Muldoon about my father and Donovan had him killed."

"Oh my God, Ruth, I'm so sorry." Olivia scooted closer to Ruth, put her arm around her shoulders, and gave her an awkward one-armed hug.

Ruth brushed the tears from her eyes and gave Olivia a weak smile. "Don't feel sorry for me. Feel sorry for Donovan Muldoon. Someday he will pay for what he did to my father. He won't see it coming. I promise you that."

There was a loud knock, and the door opened. Clyde stood in the doorway. Without saying a word, he gestured for Ruth to leave. She rose to her feet, patted Olivia on the shoulder, and hurried out the door.

Olivia curled herself into a ball in the sofa's corner, her arms around a pillow, unable to look away from this man she reviled.

"Hello, Olivia." Clyde perched on the edge of the chair. He glanced over his shoulder, then he leaned forward and rested his elbows on his knees. "Can I tell you a secret? You're not going to be here long. As soon as Declan takes care of one small thing for me, you can be on your way. One, maybe two days."

"What?" Olivia asked.

"Once Declan complies, I will release you." He pushed himself to his feet, leaned over Olivia, and brushed a lock of her hair away from her face, his fingers lingering on her cheek. "I have to tell you, Liv; I have fond memories of the two of us together. You are so very appealing."

With that statement, he left, leaving Olivia trembling with fear. She scrubbed a hand down the side of her face where he touched her. Fear made her stumble as she tried to stand up. She kept her feet beneath her long enough to crawl onto the enormous bed and surround herself with pillows in a half-hearted attempt to hide. She prayed for unconsciousness to come over her.

Chapter 21
Declan

"Declan, are you sure about this?" Drew asked. He looked his brother up and down with a critical eye. "You haven't been here since Sarah died."

Almost two years after her death and the mention of his sister's name still caused an ache in the center of Declan's chest. He missed her, and it hurt to think about her and all the potential she had. Maybe it was a bad idea to come here.

Declan stared at the small yellow house set back from the street. A large oak tree hid it from passersby. If he didn't know better, he would think someone still lived there, thanks to the exorbitant amount of money he spent on upkeep. He couldn't bring himself to let their childhood home slip into ruin.

"No, I'm not sure about this," Declan replied. He shoved open the car door and stepped out. "This is our best option, though. Clyde won't think to look for us here. After what he did to Sarah, I'm sure he thinks I won't come back here. He probably thinks I sold it or abandoned it." He took their duffel bags from the trunk and set them on the sidewalk.

Drew joined Declan on the sidewalk in front of the house. He dragged his bag over his shoulder. "We don't have to do this," he said.

"I'm fine," Declan snapped. He leaned in the car window to talk to Conor in the driver's seat. "You got this?"

Conor nodded. "I got it. I'll take care of it, don't worry." He rolled up the window, put the car in gear, and pulled away.

"Maybe I should have gone with him," Drew said.

"He'll be fine," Declan replied. "Come on. Let's go inside. You're going to tell me everything you know about the Muldoon compound."

They walked around the house to the back door. Declan reached into a crevice behind the light on the porch and grabbed the key he had hidden there years ago. He unlocked the door, and they slipped inside.

He made a phone call on the way to Boston and ensured that the house was immaculate with no dust and had mopped and vacuumed floors with a stocked refrigerator.

"Take your stuff up to your room," Declan said. "Then meet me in the kitchen so we can get started. I'm going to find a drink."

Drew hesitated at the bottom of the stairs for a split second before he trudged up them. Declan tossed his bag in the bedroom off from the living room. He avoided looking in as he passed it. The darkness filled the room, thanks to the closed blinds and covered furniture. He had no intention of entering that room ever again.

He found a bottle of whiskey in the kitchen cupboard, poured himself a glass, and downed it in two swallows. By the time Drew returned to the kitchen, Declan's head was buzzing.

Chapter 21

"Start talking," Declan ordered.

Drew proved to be a fountain of information after being held at the compound for more than a year. He shared with Declan all he knew about the Muldoon compound—people, timing, and Olivia's probable whereabouts. Declan scribbled notes in a notebook from one of the kitchen drawers, and Drew made a rough outline of a map.

Conor returned three hours after he left. He tossed a thick stack of papers on the table and smiled.

"Did you park out back?" Declan asked.

"Yeah," Conor said. "And I made sure they didn't follow me. I think we're good for now."

"And did you talk to Ruth?"

"I did. Clyde is at the compound," Conor explained. "Ruth said he came in with Olivia. The jerk left her in the car's trunk for half an hour while he chatted up his uncle. It wasn't until Donovan locked himself in his office that they moved Olivia inside. She's in a room on the north side of the mansion, west corner."

Drew nodded and tapped the sketch of the compound he'd made. "Right where I thought she would be," he said.

"How is Ruthie doing?" Declan asked.

"She's okay," Conor replied. "She fucking hates Clyde. If I asked her to stab him in his sleep, she'd do it in a heartbeat."

"What did she say about Olivia?" Declan asked.

"She's okay," Conor explained. "She told Ruth she thinks she has a concussion. Ruth said she has a bloody cut on her forehead and a bitch of a bruise on her chin."

Declan suppressed his anger. Nobody hurt Olivia and survived. If he ever got his hands on Walsh, the man would regret ever touching her. Nobody would ever hurt the woman he loved again.

"So, what's the plan?" Drew asked, interrupting Declan's unspoken fantasies of revenge.

Declan pointed at Conor. "Let's hear it."

"We have to go tonight, after midnight. Ruth said there shouldn't be more than three or four men guarding the compound. If we plan it right, we should be able to get in, get Olivia, and get out with no one knowing any better."

"Let's hope that's the case," Declan said.

"Ruth will leave the side entrance of the kitchen unlocked. We go in that way, set the charges in the kitchen, and then she'll take us up the service stairs to where they're holding Olivia. From there, it's up to us."

"Ruth has cost me a lot of money the last year," Declan said. "But she is worth every penny. Invaluable."

"She's put herself in a lot of danger working for us," Conor said. "But this time, she's risking everything. Clyde will kill her if he finds out she helped us."

Declan shook his head. "I won't let that happen. I swear I won't let anything happen to her."

"*We* won't let anything happen to her," Drew added. "I wouldn't be sitting here if it wasn't for Ruth."

"What do you mean, we?" Declan snapped. "I forbid you from going in there. You're still hurt and can barely walk."

"Declan, come on," Drew grumbled.

"Don't argue with me, damn it!" Declan stuck his finger in the younger man's chest, emphasizing each word with a stab to the heart. "I will not lose you. You are the only family I have left. You are staying here. Period."

Drew nodded. "Okay, big brother, okay. I'm sorry."

Chapter 21

Declan pushed himself away from the table. "We're leaving at midnight, Conor. I'm gonna try to get some sleep. I'm drained." He stalked down the hall to the small bedroom off the living room and slammed the door behind himself.

He sat on the edge of the bed in his childhood bedroom. His heart pounded painfully, like it might burst from his chest, and there was a low hum in his ears. He scrubbed a hand over his face, the weight of his tears heavy behind his eyes. Being home dredged up memories he didn't want to relive, especially the memory of holding his sister's dead body in his arms.

He had lost so much, had his entire world taken from him. Declan had done horrible things to save his brother, using his grief to justify the terrible things he'd done. He'd let himself become a bitter, uncaring man.

Until he walked into Olivia's bank. Something had changed in him since he'd taken Olivia as his hostage. Something came awake inside him that had long lay dormant. Olivia brought him back to life.

If he couldn't get her back, if he couldn't save her, then he had nothing left to live for anymore. Olivia was all that mattered.

Declan drove through the open gate at the back of the compound and parked the car under a stand of trees. He and Conor left the car and followed the dirt road half a mile to the mansion. They stuck to the shadows, staying away from any lights that might illuminate them. Once they reached the back of the mansion, they hid in the bushes near the back entrance.

"Where is she?" Declan grumbled. "Something is wrong. It's taking too long."

Conor checked his watch. "Give her time. It's not midnight yet. She's gotta wait until it's clear."

Declan tapped his fingers against the side of his leg. Despite the cool evening, sweat beaded on his forehead and ran down the side of his face. He needed to get inside and get to Olivia. Every minute she was inside, she was in danger.

The door opened, and Ruth stepped out. She looked in both directions before gesturing for Declan and Conor to follow her. They crowded into a cramped mud room. Ruth pressed herself against the door leading into the house, with Conor in front of her. Declan stood behind them, gun drawn, ready to enter.

"Hey, Ruthie," Conor murmured. A smile played at the corners of his mouth.

"Conor," Ruth whispered, affection clear in her voice. She squeezed his arm, then she opened the door and gestured for them to follow her down a short hallway to the kitchen.

Conor set the duffel bag over his shoulder on the floor and went to work while Declan kept watch at the door.

"How is she, Ruth?" Declan asked, afraid to hear the answer.

"Olivia's scared," Ruth replied. "But she'll never admit it. She's a tough one, that girl. You're lucky to have found her."

"Found her again," Declan muttered.

"What do you mean, again?" Ruth asked.

Declan smiled. "We dated about a million years ago, when we were much younger. Her father didn't approve of me, so Olivia broke it off."

Chapter 21

"But Conor said you kidnapped her from the last bank you robbed," Ruth said.

Declan couldn't help but chuckle. "Mere coincidence."

"Well, all I have to say is you better take care of her, Declan." Ruth stabbed her finger into the center of his chest. Despite her diminutive stature, it forced Declan to take a step back. The Scottish lilt to her voice seemed stronger thanks to her emotions. "She deserves to be protected. Make sure Clyde cannot hurt her ever again. Do you understand me?"

"Yes, ma'am," Declan said. "I didn't know you cared so much about my love life."

Ruth glared at him. "Some of us never get the chance to love someone." She shot a furtive glance in Conor's direction. "It seems you have a second chance at love with Olivia. Take advantage of that."

"I plan to," Declan said. He cleared his throat and looked away. "Conor, how's it going?"

Conor looked up from the floor next to the stove. "I think we're good." He checked his watch. "We have fifteen minutes."

"What happens in fifteen minutes?" Ruth asked.

Conor and Declan exchanged a look, then Conor made an exploding sound and spread his fingers wide.

"Boom," Conor said.

Ruth smiled. "Promise?"

"I thought you were doing this for the money, Ruthie," Declan muttered with a smile.

The petite redhead punched Declan on the shoulder. "You know this has never been about the money. That was just a bonus. But it's coming to a head, Declan, and I will be right here, watching Donovan Muldoon's world crumble around him. Which is more than he deserves. The only thing better would be his death."

Conor put his hand in the middle of Ruth's back and looked at her tenderly. "Let's see if we can make that happen."

Ruth smiled at Conor over her shoulder and pointed at a set of stairs tucked in the corner. "How about we go get your girl, Declan?"

The three of them hurried through the kitchen and up the service stairs. At the juncture where two hallways met, Ruth stopped short. She put a hand on Conor's chest and her finger to her lips, tipping her head to one side as she listened intently. She glanced at her watch.

"All right, you two, wait here," Ruth said. "I'll tell the boys outside Olivia's room that I heard something. That should get one of them down here. You two take care of them, but make sure you wait until I'm inside the room. We don't have much time before the next shift shows up, only five minutes." She picked up a small bundle of clothes from beneath one of the hall tables, straightened her dress, fluffed her hair, and gave Conor a wink. "Showtime."

Ruth hurried around the corner, her heels clicking on the hardwood floor, which drew the attention of the men guarding Olivia's door. Declan heard Ruth telling them she heard a noise in the back corridor, an unusual noise that she thought they should check out while she looked in on their guest. A few seconds later, Ruth's voice faded away, and a door closed.

Declan and Conor stepped back against the wall, into the shadows. It wasn't long before Murphy rounded the corner, his eyes widening in surprise when Conor stepped into the light. He opened his mouth to say something, but

Chapter 21

Declan coldcocked him, knocking him out. Conor caught him and lowered him to the floor.

Declan peered around the corner. Walsh leaned against the wall by the door, examining the toe of his shoe. Declan tapped Conor on the shoulder and pointed at the man passed out on the floor.

"I'm gonna move him, put him in one of these spare rooms," Declan whispered. "You take care of Walsh."

An almost evil grin spread across Conor's face, and he cracked his knuckles. "Gladly." He stalked down the hall.

Declan heard something hit the floor and several quiet curses. With two sets of zip ties from his pocket, he secured Murphy's hands and feet. He opened the nearest door, grabbed the unconscious man beneath the arms, and dragged him inside. He dumped him on the floor, ripped the tie from Murphy's neck, and used it to gag him.

Declan slipped back out the door and closed it quietly behind him. He pulled his gun from its holster and made his way down the hall, just in time to see Olivia leaving the bedroom, her hand in Ruth's.

Chapter 22
Olivia

Olivia wasn't sure why she bolted upright or what drew her attention to the bedroom door. She sat up in the middle of the bed with her head cocked, listening. A few seconds later, the door opened, and Ruth came in.

"All right, girly, this is where you get off," she whispered.

Olivia shoved the pillows surrounding her to the floor and jumped off the side of the bed. "What do you mean?"

"Put on some shoes and something warm. You're leaving."

Olivia was confused, but she did as she was told. She put on her shoes and grabbed a sweatshirt from the back of the chair, then Ruth took her hand and pulled her across the room. Ruth pressed her ear to the door and listened.

Olivia didn't know what Ruth was waiting for, but it was several minutes before she opened the door and peered out. Whatever she saw must have been to her satisfaction, because she let it fall open and pulled Olivia into the hall.

Walsh, who had been guarding her room, lay on the floor, unconscious, with Conor standing over him.

Chapter 22

Olivia gasped when she saw Conor. A second later, Declan came around the corner, his gun in his hand. He slid to a stop when he saw her.

He exhaled loudly as he strode toward her. "Olivia. Jesus, sweetheart, am I glad to see you." He wrapped her in his arms and pulled her against his chest.

Olivia sighed, clutched the lapels of his jacket, and buried her face against his chest. She needed to touch him, to feel his breath on her face, and his lips on hers. "Declan, you're here."

"Yeah, baby, in the flesh," he whispered. He ducked his head and caught her lips in his, kissing her breathless.

He was here, he was alive, and she was never letting him go again.

Ruth cleared her throat.

Declan glanced at Ruth over his shoulder, then he checked his watch. "We better go. Now. Ruthie?"

Ruth nodded. "Yes, sir." She gestured for them to follow her as she hurried down the hallway.

Declan brushed another kiss across Olivia's lips, then he took her hand as they followed Ruth through the winding maze of corridors in the house. She led them to a set of stairs, narrow and rarely used from the looks of the dust mites gathered in the corners of each step.

Ruth pointed at the narrow staircase. "There," she said. "Go down the stairs and out the door at the bottom. You'll come out the side entrance on the north side of the house." She looked behind her. "You need to hurry."

Conor squeezed Ruth's hand. "What are you doing, Ruth? You're coming with us."

Ruth took a step back. "Not this time, Conor. I need to stay here."

"Ruthie," Conor grumbled.

"It's alright, Conor," she insisted. "As long as Donovan and Clyde think I'm on their side, I'm safe."

"I don't want you to get hurt," Conor said. "You know what's about to happen."

"I'll be fine," Ruth said. She rested her hands on his chest, stood on her toes, and pressed a lingering kiss to Conor's lips. "I promise. Go. Now."

"I'm coming back for you," Conor said.

"I know." Ruth pointed a finger at Declan. "You take care of Olivia. I mean it." She turned and ran back the way they'd come.

Men stampeding through the house, doors slamming, yelling, and cursing echoed through the house. Conor turned and darted down the stairs, Declan and Olivia right behind him. Declan kept Olivia between him and Conor in their headlong rush down the stairs.

They burst through the door and stumbled down a short set of stairs. "Where's the car?" Declan asked.

Conor took a minute to get his bearing, then he pointed at the east side of the house. "That way."

"How much longer do we have?" Declan inquired.

Conor checked his watch. "It should be any minute now. We need to hurry."

They took off in a dead run. The men behind them shouted as they rounded the corner and the car came into view. Declan hustled Olivia across the lawn to the car parked beneath the trees, while Conor hung back, gun drawn and raised. When they reached the car, Declan yanked open the door and shoved Olivia inside.

"Stay down," he ordered.

"Declan—," she protested.

"I mean it, Liv." His tone left no room for argument. "Stay down." The door slammed shut.

Chapter 22

Olivia ducked behind the front seat as the sound of gunfire filled the night air. She screamed, terror flooding her like an overflowing dam. Her first instinct was to throw open the door and run to Declan. She saw his muscled back and broad shoulders through the window above her head and heard him shouting orders at Conor.

She slapped her hands over her ears and cringed when another burst of gunfire erupted near the car. Declan and Conor dropped to the ground as gunfire came from every direction and bullets hit the car. Olivia ducked her head and tried to make herself as small as possible.

A sudden explosion rocked the car, breaking all the windows and showering her in glass. Olivia pushed herself to her knees as another blast shook the car. She peered out the cracked back window. The night sky was lit up like the sun had risen and heat rolled across the dew- sprinkled lawn. The sounds of fear, anger, and pain echoed through the night air.

Declan opened the back door and fell inside. He grabbed Olivia and shoved her beneath him, using his body to shield her.

"Go, Conor!" he shouted.

Even though one door was still hung open, Conor started the car and drove. The car jerked, as if it didn't want to go, before it gained speed and flew down the road. The tires squealed as they rounded the corner at breakneck speed.

Declan sat up, grabbed the open door, and yanked it shut. Olivia climbed to her knees and stared out the window, watching as the bright orange sky faded behind them.

They pulled off the road into an empty parking lot fifteen miles from the Muldoon compound. Conor parked in the back, away from the streetlights. He put the car in park and turned to look at Declan.

"Is everyone okay?" Declan asked.

Conor touched his arm and winced. "Bullet grazed me." He reached into the glove compartment, removed a purple handkerchief, and tied it around his upper arm. "But I'll live."

"Olivia?" Declan turned to her and ran his hands over her body, searching for injuries.

"I'm fine," she whispered.

Declan kissed her, then he pulled his phone from his pocket. A scowl marred his face when he read the screen.

"We can't go back to the house," Declan said.

"Why not?" Conor asked. "What happened?"

Declan held his phone up and pointed at it. "Drew called. He said he noticed the same car drive past the house four or five times, then it parked up the street. He waited two hours for them to leave and when they didn't, he grabbed everything he could, loaded it into the SUV, and took off."

"Where's he going?" Conor asked.

"Wakefield. He's got a friend there that has an empty rental property he said we can use. It's furnished, and no one has been using it for weeks. He's going to meet his friend there. He's texting me the address."

"We need to ditch the car," Conor said. "If a cop sees us, we're in deep shit."

"We're gonna have to steal another car," Declan said.

Chapter 22

"On it." Conor climbed out of the car and took off down the street at a slow jog. He disappeared around the corner after a few seconds.

Declan turned to Olivia. He brushed her cheek with the back of his hand. "Are you okay?" he whispered.

"I … I think so. No major injuries. A few scrapes and bruises, but otherwise, I'm fine. What about you?"

"Same." He held out his arms. "Come here."

Olivia slid across the seat and fell into Declan's arms. She buried her face against his chest and breathed deeply. He smelled like leather and gunpowder. She loved it.

"Clyde said he was going to let me go after you did something for him. What did he mean?" Her voice sounded muffled, since her face was pressed against his chest.

"It's a long story, but in short, he was going to let all of us go free if I did one thing for him. Except that one thing probably would have gotten me—us—killed. I have other plans." Declan kissed the top of her head.

Olivia sighed. "It's not over, is it?"

"No, it's not. Not yet, anyway."

A loud honk came from across the lot. Out the window, Olivia saw Conor parked in a beat-up, old pickup truck.

"Let's go," Declan said. "We need to make ourselves scarce."

The rental property was on the edge of Wakefield, situated back off the street, far away from the other homes. They parked the car in the garage, and Conor moved the SUV several blocks away.

The house was large with two stories, four bedrooms, and a large, enclosed patio that wrapped around the back of the house.

That was where Oliva found Declan an hour after they arrived, stretched out on an extra-large, dark blue chaise lounge. One foot rested on the floor, he held a glass of whiskey in his hand with the bottle on the floor beside him. The smell of burning wood rose from the stove in the corner, and the quiet pop of the logs breaking apart filled her ears.

"Declan?" she murmured.

He didn't even turn his head, just held out his hand, gesturing for her to join him. Olivia hesitated for a second because she was half-naked, wearing one of Declan's old T-shirts over her underwear. She had found a large blanket in the hall closet and wrapped it around herself.

"It's warm over here," Declan said. "That old wood-burning stove works great." He patted the chaise lounge and moved over so she could lie down next to him. It was wide enough that both fit comfortably on it. He draped his arm over her legs and pulled her close.

"How's Conor?" he asked.

She sighed. "He's okay. The bullet only grazed him. Once I cleaned and disinfected it, it didn't even need stitches. I put a nice, tight bandage on it to staunch the bleeding. He's upstairs drinking himself to sleep."

The bullet that grazed Conor dug a long groove into his upper arm that looked far worse than it was. Conor was an ideal patient; he sat quietly as Olivia cleaned and bandaged the wound. When she finished, he squeezed her hand and thanked her.

It surprised Olivia that Conor's injury was the worst any of them suffered. Olivia didn't have a mark on her,

Chapter 22

and Declan had a few cuts from flying glass. He also had a bullet hole the size of a coin in the bottom of his jacket.

"Where's Drew?" Declan asked. His fingers drifted up and down her bare leg, which sent shivers up and down her spine.

"He's asleep upstairs too," Olivia replied. "I looked in on him, but he didn't even stir." She cupped Declan's cheek in her hand and brushed her thumb over his lips. "Thank you for coming to my rescue."

Declan scowled. "Clyde should never have been able to get you."

Olivia silenced him with a kiss. When she pulled away, she rested her forehead against his and breathed him in. They were alive, and they were together. That was all that mattered.

Declan slipped his hand into her hair and pulled her close. He kissed her, a brush of his lips over hers, enough to send tingles of desire shooting through every nerve ending. He shifted so he could drop his glass of whiskey to the floor, then he slid both arms around her and pulled her flush against his body.

A shiver raced through her, though she wasn't sure if it was because of Declan's touch or the frosty night air.

"Are you okay?" he asked.

"Just a little cold," she replied. She cupped his cheek. "Declan, I ... I want to tell you something."

Declan shook his head. "Tell me when this is over."

A tear slipped down Olivia's cheek. "What if I don't get the chance?"

He rested his forehead against hers. "You will. I promise."

Olivia closed her eyes. "I'm holding you to that promise, Declan Quinn." She pressed her face to the side of his neck and breathed him in.

"Please don't let anything happen to him," she silently prayed. "Please."

Chapter 23

Olivia

Olivia shut the bedroom door and sat on the edge of the bed. She stared at the cell phone in her hand, still unsure if she really wanted to make the call. It had been over three years since they had spoken; she wasn't even sure Caitlin would answer.

Two days earlier, Declan had gotten everyone cell phones. Olivia shoved hers into the bottom of a bag of clothes with no intention of ever using it. She didn't need it; she had no one to call. An hour ago, Declan sat next to her at the kitchen table and took her hand.

"Call your sister," he whispered. He slid her phone across the table.

"Where did you find that?" Olivia mumbled.

"In the bag of clothes in the closet. Liv, look at me."

She reluctantly lifted her head and looked into his mesmerizing green eyes. "What?"

"I know you miss your family," Declan said.

Olivia narrowed her eyes. "Yes, I miss them. I haven't seen them in three years. But I don't need to call them."

Declan leaned his head against hers. "You talk in your sleep, baby. You miss your sister. Call her. A quick phone call to tell her you're okay."

Olivia sighed. "Are you sure?"

"Yes." He kissed her cheek. "Make it quick though, okay?"

She had picked up the phone and closed herself in the bedroom. It was so easy, just one phone call to hear Caitlin's voice and tell her she was alive and well. What was the harm?

"Screw it," Olivia mumbled. She quickly dialed the number she had memorized when she was a teenager and held the phone to her ear. She held her breath as it rang.

"Hello?" a female voice answered.

Olivia exhaled. It was her, Caitlin O'Reilly, her younger sister. The last time Olivia saw her, she was barely nineteen, and now she was twenty-two and doing God-knows-what.

"Hello?" Caitlin repeated. "Look, you have about five seconds to say something before I hang up. I don't have time for this crap."

"Caitlin, it's me," Olivia blurted out.

Caitlin sighed. "Me, who?" she asked.

"It's Liv," she said. "Your sister."

Caitlin was silent for too long. Olivia checked the phone to see if they had disconnected, but they hadn't. She tried to think of something to say, but Caitlin spoke first.

"Jesus, Liv, you're alive?" her sister blurted out.

"You thought I was dead?" Olivia asked.

"I didn't know what to think," Caitlin said. "Daddy couldn't get any information out of the Muldoons, and nobody has heard from you for three years." Caitlin sucked in a deep breath. "Holy shit! It is so good to hear your voice."

Olivia laughed. "It's good to hear yours too. How are you? How are Mom and Dad?"

Chapter 23

Caitlin snorted. "I think you're the one who needs to be answering questions, big sister. Like, where the hell are you? Where have you been for three years? Most importantly, when are you coming home?"

Olivia sighed. That was the one question she hoped Caitlin wouldn't ask. Because, honestly, she didn't know if she could ever go home. She took a deep breath.

"I don't know if I *am* coming home," she said. "There are a lot of things going on, things that I can't explain."

"That's not an answer," Caitlin interrupted. "Do you know what we've gone through since you disappeared? It has been hell around here."

Olivia rolled her eyes. "Don't guilt-trip me, Caitlin. You don't know what *I* went through, what I endured for the sake of my family. I had no choice but to disappear. I know you might not understand that, but I did what I had to do. It wasn't easy and yes, people got hurt. Shit, people *died* because of me, but I had to do it. Otherwise, I would probably be dead myself."

"Liv, what happened?" Caitlin whispered. "You have to tell me."

"I will, I swear," Olivia promised. "But not yet, not today. I just … I just really wanted to hear your voice. I miss you."

"Same, sis," Caitlin murmured. She cleared her throat. "Okay, I'll wait to hear what happened, but I'm holding you to your promise. You will tell me."

"You got it," Olivia said. "Look, I have to go. Please don't tell Mom and Dad I called."

"But, Mom—."

"Please, Caitlin. I know I'm asking a lot, but I need you to promise me you won't tell them. Not yet anyway. It shouldn't be long now. Then I can explain everything."

"Okay," Caitlin said. "I promise."

Olivia swallowed around the lump in her throat. "I love you, Caitlin. Take care of yourself, okay?"

"I will," Caitlin said. "I love you, too."

Olivia disconnected the call. She closed her eyes and took a deep breath. It had to be over soon.

Please let it be over soon.

Olivia lay sprawled across the bed, with Declan's head on her stomach. His finger traced circles on her inner thigh and every few minutes, he would turn his head and press a kiss to her hip, humming contentedly in the back of his throat.

She brushed her fingers through his hair and smiled to herself. It was nice to have some time alone with him. They had been staying at the rental property in Wakefield for a week, all four of them—her, Declan, Drew, and Conor—constantly bumping into each other. On the seventh day they were there, Drew and Conor left them alone for the evening. They hadn't said where they were going, but they'd vowed to stay gone for hours.

"I'm starving," she mumbled. Olivia pushed herself out from underneath Declan, giggling when he tried to keep her on the bed. She grabbed his shirt from the floor and pulled it on.

"I need to get some clothes," she said. "I'm getting fed up with wearing the same thing day after day."

"Come back to bed," said Declan. He scrambled to his feet, pulled her into his arms, and nuzzled her neck with his nose.

Chapter 23

Olivia stepped out of his arms with a sigh. "I am hungry. Come with me. I think I saw some leftover pie." She took his hand and tried to drag him with her.

Declan laughed and pointed at his naked body. "I need pants. I'll be right there."

Olivia was cutting the pie and putting it on plates by the time Declan emerged from the bedroom. True to his word, he had put on pants and a red T-shirt. He came up behind her, rested his hands on her waist, and kissed her neck. She relaxed against him, her eyes slipping closed as she let herself get lost in the feel of Declan touching her and kissing her.

Declan's hands painfully clamped down on her waist, and the kiss abruptly ended as his lips flattened into a thin line.

"Do not move, and do not make a sound."

Her entire body went stiff, and her hands shook at the sound of Walsh's voice. She pressed a hand to her lips to stifle the scream rising in her throat.

"Turn around, Olivia," Walsh said. "Nice and slow."

Declan took a step back, and Olivia turned with the knife covered in pie remnants still clutched in her hand. Walsh stared at her over Declan's shoulder, with his gun pointed at the back of Declan's head.

"Drop the knife on the counter," Walsh ordered. "Do it now or I will shoot him. I don't think you want his brains splattered across your face."

Olivia swallowed, the taste in her mouth coppery and thick. "N-no," she stuttered. "Pl-please don't." She dropped the knife on the counter and held up her hands.

Walsh brought the gun down hard on the back of Declan's head. He slumped to the floor at her feet. Before she could move, Walsh's hand was on her throat, cutting off her scream, along with her airway. Her mouth dropped open as she tried to drag in a breath. She clawed at Walsh's hands.

A smile spread across Walsh's face. "Save your screams for later, honey," he whispered. "You'll need them."

Olivia didn't want to scream; she didn't want to cry, but the pain was worse than any she had ever experienced. Walsh started with slaps and punches all over her body, laughing every time his fist connected with any part of her. She struggled to get away, but the ropes tying her to the furniture in the small front living room were too tight. Fighting against the bindings only made them tighter.

She opened her eyes. Declan sat against the wall on the other side of the room, forced to watch everything Walsh did to her. He was the reason she didn't want to scream; the agony on Declan's face terrified her. Maybe if she didn't scream, it wouldn't be so bad.

Walsh slapped her so hard, her face bounced against the hardwood floors and tears leaked from her eyes. Declan grunted and closed his eyes. That was when Walsh took out the knife and dragged it down her leg, from her inner thigh to her knee, a shallow but painful cut. She couldn't help it; a high-pitched, keening sound erupted from her.

Declan's eyes shot open. Walsh darted across the room and punched Declan in the kidneys. Then he grabbed Declan's hair and forced him to look at Olivia. He mumbled something Olivia couldn't hear, something that made Declan look ready to kill.

Chapter 23

"Let her go," she heard Declan say. "Let her go, and I might let you live."

Walsh laughed and returned to Olivia's side. He took the knife out and went to work. He knew what he was doing. Each cut was deep enough to hurt, yet shallow enough to keep the blood loss to a minimum. He intended to kill her slowly. She screamed each time the knife penetrated her skin, and the blood oozed from the cut. Just when she thought she couldn't take another second of the pain, Walsh would stop, long enough for her to catch her breath. Then it would start again.

The coppery scent of her own blood filled her nostrils, and her screams echoed in her head. Blackness overtook her vision. She didn't fight it.

The next time she opened her eyes, Declan was on the floor, crawling across the room in some kind of bizarre army crawl. Her heart pounded.

"Declan, no, he'll kill you," she mumbled.

Declan ignored her and continued across the room. He was going toward the sideboard by the wall where he had stashed weapons. She dragged in a deep breath, but the effort was too much for her. Olivia closed her eyes and let the darkness take her.

Chapter 24
Declan

It was every nightmare Declan ever had manifested right in front of him. Walsh sprawled Olivia out on the floor, her arms tied to the couch and her legs spread wide, tied to the coffee table. Walsh shoved the other furniture out of the way and forced Declan to sit on the other side of the room against the wall. He couldn't move with his hands and feet tied, but he could see everything Walsh did to Olivia.

The first time Walsh hurt her, Declan closed his eyes, but then he heard a terrified, keening sound coming from Olivia. He opened his eyes to see Walsh dragging a knife from her inner thigh to her knee, blood trickling to the floor from the cut.

Walsh stalked across the room, punched him in the kidneys, then he grabbed Declan's hair and forced him to look at Olivia.

"Keep your eyes open, Declan," Walsh ordered. "You will watch every second of this. Clyde's orders. If you turn away or close your eyes for even one second, I hurt you first, then I hurt her."

"Let her go," Declan snarled. "Let her go and I might let you live."

Chapter 24

Walsh laughed, the sound filling the room and echoing off the wall. Olivia stared at him as he returned to her side, her eyes wide and frightened. Blood ran down her leg, tears streaked her face, and her sobs filled the room.

Declan's stomach clenched, and vomit rose in the back of his throat as the knife penetrated Olivia's skin. He had promised to protect her and keep her safe. He failed her.

After a while, Olivia stopped screaming, her voice cutting off with a strangled cry. Only then did Walsh take a step back. Bruises bloomed all over Olivia's body, blood dripped from the cuts he had inflicted, her eyes were closed, and her mouth slack. Walsh brushed a hand across his forehead, leaving a grotesque line of blood on his forehead. He turned to Declan.

"I think she needs a break, don't you?" Walsh sneered, as he crouched in front of Declan with his arms resting on his knees. "I'm going to give her a chance to catch her breath. If I'm lucky, she'll wake up. I like to see her pretty eyes when she's begging me to stop." He stood up, eyed Olivia up and down one more time, then he picked up a bottle of whiskey from the table and took a long drink. "I could use some sustenance too, you know? You stay right there, Deck. I'll be back." His laughter drifted back over his shoulder, as he walked down the hall toward the back of the house.

As soon as Walsh's footsteps faded away, Declan rolled to his stomach and used his elbows to drag himself across the floor. He kept his eyes on Olivia as he moved.

Though she was on the verge of unconsciousness, she watched him with half-open eyes, glazed over in pain. Blood, tears, and snot covered her face and her chest heaved with the effort of breathing. Gore streaked her body, and blood and sweat matted her hair to her face.

"Declan, no," she whispered, her words barely discernible. "He'll kill you."

He shook his head. If he didn't do something, Olivia would die. There was no doubt in his mind that Walsh would kill Olivia and make Declan watch. Clyde knew it would destroy him, so Declan wasn't about to let it happen.

He reached the sideboard on the other side of the room, pushed himself to his knees, and braced his bound hands against the wall. As he tried to stand up, he prayed Walsh wouldn't hear a thing. He twisted awkwardly and leaned on the doorjamb with one shoulder. His feet slipped on the hardwood floor, so it took him a second to get his balance.

Once he had his feet under him, he slid open the drawer, pushed aside the linens inside, and searched until he found what he wanted. A sigh of relief escaped him as his fingers found the knife, one of many weapons hidden throughout the house. He pulled it free, but it fell from his hands. He dropped to one knee and caught it before it hit the floor. The sharp edge sliced two of his fingers, so his blood dripped onto the floor.

Declan glanced at Olivia, but her eyes were closed and her breathing so shallow he wasn't even sure she *was* breathing. He couldn't see her chest rising and falling. His heart stuttered in his chest.

"Olivia?" he whispered. "Liv, wake up, please. Stay with me."

She didn't move, not even a twitch.

Declan growled. He twisted the knife in his hand and sawed at the rope binding his wrists. Almost dropping the knife again, he bit his lip to suppress his cry as his

Chapter 24

fingers slipped on the blood-coated handle. He closed his eyes and listened intently for Walsh's footsteps in the hallway. When he didn't appear, Declan took a deep breath and concentrated. It only took a few more swipes of the knife before the rope fell to the floor. He sat down and cut his legs free, then he was back on his feet. He looked around the corner just in time to see Walsh's back as he walked from the kitchen into the small bedroom Declan and Olivia shared.

Despite the horrific pain working its way through his bruised and battered body, Declan moved to Olivia's side. As much as he wanted to kill Walsh, he had to make sure Olivia was alive. He patted her cheek gently, praying she would respond.

"Hey Liv, look at me, baby," he whispered.

Olivia's eyes fluttered. She opened them and focused on Declan.

"Hi, baby." He kissed the corner of her mouth. "That's my girl. I will be right back, okay? I promise."

She shook her head and whispered, "No."

Declan kissed her again, the coppery smell of her blood assaulting him. It fueled his anger. "I promise, Liv. I will be right back."

In the same drawer as the knife, Declan had stashed a gun. He checked to make sure the gun was loaded, but before he could slip down the hall after Walsh, he heard a car pulling into the driveway. He glanced out the window to see the black SUV coming to a stop in front of the house.

"Shit," Declan cursed under his breath.

Footsteps thundered through the house as Walsh ran down the hall, headed back to the living room, drawn by the sound of the car. Declan stepped back and hid in the shadows against the wall. When Walsh crossed the threshold into the room, Declan slashed out with the knife, nicking Walsh's arm as he rushed past.

Walsh screamed, though Declan wasn't sure if it was out of pain or anger. It didn't matter either way because it slowed him down long enough for Declan to tackle him, taking his legs out from underneath him. They fell to the floor, both of them grunting and fighting for dominance. Walsh pushed Declan off him, knocking him back onto his ass, the gun and knife falling out of his hands.

The front door opened, and shouts of surprise filled the room when Drew and Conor saw the scene in front of them. Drew froze while Conor rushed to help Declan with Walsh.

"Conor, you and Drew get Liv out of here!" Declan yelled.

Walsh tried to stand up, but Declan lunged forward and grabbed his foot. Walsh fell to his knees.

"What about you?" Conor yelled, as he sprinted across the room to Olivia's side.

"Forget about me," Declan said. "Get her out of here."

"Touch her and you fucking die, Sullivan," Walsh yelled.

"Andrew, now!" Declan didn't care what happened to him as long as they got Olivia out.

Drew seemed to wake up, darted across the living room, and set to work helping Conor untie Olivia. When they finished, Conor scooped her into his arms and rushed out the front door, with Drew right behind him.

Walsh cursed, turned around, and punched Declan, his fist connecting with Declan's chin, rocking his head back. Declan lost his grip on Walsh, allowing him to break free. Walsh scrambled across the floor on his hands and knees, trying to get to the door.

Chapter 24

With an unearthly scream, Declan pushed himself to his feet, picked the gun up off the floor, then he slammed Walsh to the floor, his entire body covering the other man. Walsh fought to get free, to get the advantage. He grabbed Declan's shoulders and flipped him to his back. Walsh reached for the gun, wrapped a hand around Declan's wrist and another around the butt of the weapon.

The two men fought, grunts and curses filling the room as they each vied for control of the weapon.

Declan heard the gun go off, though nothing registered for a few seconds, time frozen as he waited for the inevitable pain, the blood, the release, the end.

But there was nothing.

Instead, Walsh's eyes widened, and his mouth went slack. His head fell back and hit the floor. He gasped once, then nothing.

Declan rolled to his side, pushing himself away from Walsh's dead body. He was out of breath, and every muscle in his body screamed in agony. Trying to muster enough strength to move, he groaned. He needed to get to Olivia.

"Declan!"

Conor appeared out of nowhere and helped Declan to his feet. He pulled one of Declan's arms over his shoulder and half-walked, half-dragged Declan out the front door.

"Olivia?" Declan mumbled.

"She's alive," Conor said. "Barely. Drew is in the car with her. We need to get her to a doctor."

Declan nodded in silent agreement. Conor got him to the SUV, opened the door, and lowered him to the seat beside Olivia. Declan reached for her, pulling her nearly lifeless body into his arms, her head on his chest tucked under his chin. His hand rested on her chest, in the space between her breasts. He needed to feel her breathe, feel the rise and fall of her chest, and feel her heart beating beneath his hand. He would hold her and will her to stay alive until they could get her to a hospital. His heart pounded in fear.

"Don't leave me, Olivia," he begged. "You cannot leave me."

Conor got behind the wheel and backed out of the driveway so fast he hit the mailbox and knocked it to the ground. He cursed under his breath as he turned the wheel and took off as fast as the car would allow.

"We need to get Olivia to a doctor," Declan said. "Then we call Shane."

Conor glanced at Declan in the rearview mirror, his brow furrowed in concern. "Shane?" he asked. "You're going to call Shane Kelly? Deck, he's crazy."

"Shane is exactly what we need," Declan snapped. "I am done. We have to end this. I will not let Clyde Braniff live long enough to hurt Olivia again. Shane is crazy enough to help me stop him. I have no choice."

"Whatever you say, boss," Conor mumbled. "Whatever you say."

Chapter 25
Olivia

Olivia dreamed of men with guns and knives, blood, pain, and death. Declan appeared intermittently, never completely there, as he tried to save her from the monster stalking her. Someone called her name, imploring her to wake up and look at him.

Olivia blinked several times, unsure why the room wouldn't come into focus. She closed her eyes and took a deep breath. She shifted and tried to put her arms above her head, wanting to stretch and release the aches in her body. Instead, excruciating pain overwhelmed her, the ache so deep in her muscles and bones that it brought tears to her eyes. She grabbed her arm and moaned as more pain bit deep into her. There wasn't any place on her body that didn't hurt.

"Olivia?" The voice a foot above her head was familiar. "Olivia, can you hear me?"

She squinted and waited for the owner of the voice to swim into focus.

"Conor?" Olivia croaked. Her voice was raspy and unused.

"Yeah, it's me. Thank God you're awake."

Olivia lifted her head and tried to ignore the excessive pounding behind her eyes. She peered at the man hovering over her. He was alone.

"Where's Declan?" she whispered. Fear made her gut clench in agony. What if Walsh killed Declan, or he sacrificed himself to save her?

Conor crossed the room and pushed the door closed, then he returned to Olivia's side. He sat in the chair next to the bed, took her hand, and gently squeezed it. "He's safe, Olivia. Safe and alive," he said. "It's just ... he can't be here."

Olivia narrowed her eyes. "I don't understand," she whispered. "Why can't he be here?" A tear slid down her cheek, but it hurt too much to wipe it away.

"Aside from being the most wanted man on the East Coast? Well, Walsh is dead, Liv. Declan shot him," Conor explained. "The police have been coming around, asking a million questions about you."

"What did you tell them?" she asked. "Do they know what happened to Walsh? Do they know it was Declan?"

"They don't know any of that. I told them I found you wandering down the side of the road, bloody and cut up, so I picked you up and brought you here."

"They believed you?" Olivia asked.

"I don't know," Conor said. "I think I play the good Samaritan pretty well. As far as anybody knows, I'm just some guy who found a woman on the side of the road and helped her out. The nurses think I'm this great guy because I keep coming around to check on you. I'm pretty sure I could get a date without even trying."

"Ruth would kill you," she croaked. She gestured to the water on the bedside table.

Chapter 25

Conor smiled as he got to his feet and poured water in a plastic cup. He put a straw in it, then he hit the button to raise her bed. Once she was upright, he held the cup for her while she took a drink.

"You're right, Ruth would kill me." He set the cup on the tray at the foot of the bed.

Olivia cleared her throat. "The police haven't connected what happened to me with what happened to Walsh?"

Conor shook his head. "No. It took the cops two days to find Walsh. Drew's friend, uh, George something, called it in. He said he went to check on his rental property and found a dead body in the house. Before he called them, we went through that place and got rid of anything that might implicate us. No fingerprints, no blood, nothing. As far as the cops know, George found a dead body, and nobody knows why or what happened."

"Thank God. Wait, do they know who I am?" she asked.

"No, you're registered as Jane Doe. I brought you in with no purse, no belongings, nothing." Conor shifted in his chair. "Look, Liv, the cops want to talk to you. You probably shouldn't tell them you're Liv O'Reilly."

"God, no," she said. "As far as anyone knows, I'm Olivia Miller. If anybody finds out I'm Liv O'Reilly, word could get back to my father. I do not want my family dragged into this shit with Clyde. I don't want them to get hurt." She pinched the bridge of her nose and closed her eyes. "This is a nightmare. What the hell am I supposed to tell them?"

Conor shrugged. "I wish I knew. Whatever you tell them cannot connect to Declan or Walsh or any of us."

Olivia's chest tightened, and she couldn't breathe. Trapped in a never-ending loop of insanity, she yearned for an escape. She was sick of running, sick of hiding, sick of all the lies she constantly had to tell. She couldn't handle much more.

Connor offered her a tissue, which she readily took. "Will you tell Declan I miss him?" she asked.

"I will, Liv," Conor said. He squeezed her hand. "We'll take care of this, I promise."

"I know," Olivia replied. "I just, well, I won't feel safe until Declan is by my side."

"Trust me, he feels the same way. He is driving me nuts with all the questions and the instructions." Conor looked at his watch. "I better go. Now that you're awake, the police will come around." He patted her hand. "We'll get you out of here as soon as we can." He smiled and disappeared out the door.

The doctor spent almost an hour with her, discussing her injuries and assessing her recovery. By the time he left, Olivia could barely keep her eyes open. Unfortunately, five minutes after he left, a female police officer tapped on the door and stepped into her room.

"Mind if I come in?" she asked.

"Sure." Olivia sighed and adjusted her bed so she could sit up more. "What can I do for you, officer?"

"Willet, Officer Willet," the young woman replied. She stepped into the room and took a notebook from her pocket. "How are you feeling, ma'am?"

Olivia smiled. "I'm okay," she said.

"Glad to hear it." Officer Willet was all business. She marched across the room and sat in the chair beside Olivia's bed. "I'll try to make this quick. Your name, ma'am?"

Chapter 25

"Olivia Miller."

Officer Willet looked at her over the top of her glasses, one eyebrow raised. "Miller? Okay." She scribbled in her notebook. "Address?"

Olivia closed her eyes, searching her memory for the address she had used in Pennsylvania. It took her a second to remember it, but once it came to her, she gave it to the officer.

"You're not from here?" Willet said.

"No, I'm not," Olivia replied. "I was in town for a job interview."

"Do you remember what happened? Can you tell me how you got injured?"

Olivia had thought long and hard about what she would say when asked this question. She had to be careful not to let them know who she was, or that she knew Declan Quinn.

"After my interview, I was trying to find a bus stop or a cab or something, and I think I got turned around. Lost." She sighed. "I remember a lot of brick buildings, industrial buildings, but not much else. I stopped to fix my shoe, and then the next thing I remember was waking up in the hospital."

"You didn't see anybody or anything?" Officer Willet asked.

"If I did, I don't remember," Olivia said. "Everything is kind of a blur."

"Your injuries suggest you were tortured. You don't remember any of that?"

Walsh's leering grin flashed through Olivia's head, making her shudder. She swallowed and when she spoke, her voice was barely above a whisper.

"It was a man, a horrible man. I ... I think he enjoyed hurting me. It was awful." Olivia squeezed the blanket in her hands. "I wish I could remember, Officer Willet, I really do. Whoever did this to me should be punished, Officer Willet. I'm sorry; it's all a blank."

Willet nodded. "Your doctor said that might be a possibility. Amnesia brought on by a traumatic experience. I thought maybe if we talked, it might jog your memory."

"I'm sorry I can't be more help," Olivia murmured.

Officer Willet shut her notebook, sat back in her chair, and crossed her legs. She stared at Olivia for so long she felt uncomfortable.

"You know, you look familiar," Willet said.

Olivia smiled. "I have one of those faces. People always think they know me, but it turns out they don't." She shrugged one shoulder, wincing when a twinge of pain shot down her back.

"No, it's not that. I'm sure I've seen you before. Have you ever been to the Boston area before?" Willet asked.

Olivia shook her head, regretting it when a jolt of pain shot through her head and neck. "No, never."

"Hmm." Willet shook her head. "I just can't shake the idea that I know you."

Olivia sighed. "Like I said, I have one of those faces. Now, if you don't have any more questions, officer, I'd like to get some sleep."

Officer Willet gave her a tender smile, then she leaned forward, her elbows on her knees. "I like you, Olivia. I know I don't know you, but there's something about you that makes me want to help you." Her voice dropped to a low whisper. "You seem like someone who needs help. You can talk to me, it's okay. I can protect you."

Chapter 25

Olivia had to bite her tongue to keep from laughing. It was almost cute how this young cop thought she could protect Olivia. If only she knew what she would be up against if she tried.

"Thank you, Officer Willet—."

"Rose. You can call me Rose."

Olivia smiled. "I appreciate everything, *Rose*, really, but I don't need help. I don't know who hurt me or why. I'm sorry, but I'm not able to help you."

Willet got up, took a business card from her pocket, and set it on the table. "If you change your mind, my cell phone number is on there. Call me anytime." She moved to the door and put her hand on the knob. She looked over her shoulder at Olivia. "I mean it. Anytime. You take care of yourself, Ms. O'Reilly." The door closed behind her.

Olivia stared after her. "I think I underestimated you, Officer Willet," she whispered.

Chapter 26
Declan

Declan paced the fifteen-by-fifteen-foot room, unable to sit still for more than a few minutes. They holed up in a shithole above a bar on the outskirts of Boston for days, waiting for Olivia to wake up. He couldn't sleep or eat. Whiskey and water were his go-to instead of food.

It killed Declan that he couldn't be with her, sitting by her, holding her hand while she recovered. He despised the fact that she was in the hospital room, alone, with no one to watch over her. Conor did his best, but he was a poor substitute for the man who loved her. The hospital staff kept him on a short leash, especially since he supposedly didn't know her. Declan worried that Clyde's men would find her and kill her. He couldn't rest until he got her out of the hospital and back with him.

Declan was waiting for word from Shane Kelly, his so-called crazy friend. They couldn't safely move until Shane gave him the okay, which was why he hadn't gotten Olivia out of that hospital yet. Two hours earlier, Shane sent one of his men to tell Declan they were ready; it was time to move.

Conor came through the door. "Olivia talked to the police."

Chapter 26

Declan stopped pacing and ran a hand through his hair. "When? What happened?"

"This morning," Conor said. "Olivia thought everything was fine, but when the cop left, she called her Ms. O'Reilly."

Declan froze. "What?"

"The cop knew Liv," Conor continued. "Called her Ms. O'Reilly."

"What did Liv do?" Declan asked.

Conor shrugged. "Nothing. She said that the cop is harmless, maybe a little ambitious, but she thinks she'll keep quiet."

Declan shook his head. "I hope she's right. But if somebody knows who she is, then we need to get Liv out of that hospital." Declan poured himself more whiskey. "How is she?"

"She's in pain," Conor replied. "Doc says she has a concussion, and he's worried about the blood loss and how it might have affected her. She's weak, and it hurts every time she moves. Walsh did a number on her."

Declan grimaced. "That's why he's dead. It will be a cold day in hell before I let anybody hurt the woman I love again. I'm done playing the fool. Walsh got what he deserved, and Clyde will too. I guarantee it."

Conor nodded. "The doctor wants to keep her for at least two days. She argued with him, but he's insistent."

"Dammit," Declan mumbled. He sat in the nearest chair and put his head in his hands. "I heard from Shane. He's ready for us. We can't afford for Liv to be in that place for two more days. We have to move now."

"She could check herself out against the doctor's advice—."

"No." Declan shook his head. "That might raise a red flag with that young, ambitious police officer. All we need is some overzealous cop on the hunt for Olivia Miller, a woman who doesn't exist. We'll go get her. Tonight."

"How the hell are we supposed to do that?" Conor asked.

"I don't know yet, but I'll figure something out. Find Drew." Declan shoved himself to his feet. "We have work to do."

Visiting hours ended two hours before they arrived, which was exactly what Declan wanted. Hospitals were notoriously easy to enter, thanks to the dozens of entrances that were left unguarded. Nobody thought to watch for an open door of a hospital. It should be easy to walk in and get to Olivia's room. Getting her out would be the hard part.

It was easy to get in, just as Declan thought. He and Drew walked through an open side door next to the parking lot while Conor waited in the car. They didn't see anyone until they got to the nurse's station on Olivia's floor. A lone nurse sat in front of a computer, her back to them as she typed, her head bobbing to the music coming from a pair of wireless headphones in her ears.

"Stay here," Declan whispered.

Drew nodded and eased into the shadows in the hall. Declan checked the room numbers, noting Olivia's room was on his side of the nurse's station. He moved quietly to her door and slipped inside.

Olivia slept on her back, her arms at her side, bandages covering both arms and an IV in the back of her hand. Dark purple bruises covered her neck and upper

Chapter 26

chest. Declan couldn't see her legs, but he could imagine how they looked after what Walsh had done to her. Seeing her like this made him want to kill Walsh all over again.

Declan walked across the room and took her hand. He brushed the hair from her face and leaned down to whisper in her ear. "Olivia? Liv, honey, wake up."

Her eyes popped open, almost as if she had been waiting for him. "Declan," she mumbled. "Is that you?"

"Yeah, *macushla*, it's me," he replied. "You ready to get out of this place?"

Olivia nodded and clutched his hand. "God, yes." She struggled to sit up, moaning as her muscles clenched in protest at the abrupt movement.

Declan shook his head. "Wait a second. I need to get all this stuff off you. The nurse is going to come running when I pull the heart monitor, so I need you to do exactly as I say. Do you understand me?"

"Yes," Olivia murmured.

Declan removed the IV from her hand, then he helped her sit up and wrapped a blanket around her. The last thing he did was pull the sensors off her chest. Within seconds, the machine beeped, alerting the nurse something was wrong. Declan gathered Olivia in his arms and headed for the door. It opened just as he got there.

Drew stood in front of him, the nurse they had seen earlier wrapped tight in his arms, Drew's hand over her mouth. He pushed past Declan, shoved the nurse in the bathroom, slammed the door shut, and propped a chair under the handle, making it impossible to open.

"We need to hurry," Drew said. "I don't think that will hold her for long."

"I can walk," Olivia muttered.

"No, I got you," Declan said. He held her in his arms, hugging her to his chest. He kissed the top of her head, then he nodded at Drew. "Lead the way, bro."

They rushed through the hospital, closed doors flying by on either side of them. They burst out the door they had come in, Drew holding it open as Declan exited with Olivia in his arms.

Conor started the car as Drew opened the back door and Declan climbed inside, Olivia's slight form in his arms. The door slammed shut, and Drew got into the front with Conor. The tires squealed on the pavement as they left the hospital parking lot.

Declan held Olivia in his arms, his lips pressed to her forehead, breathing her in while Conor drove them into the night.

Once Declan had Olivia settled in a bedroom upstairs, he went to find Shane. He'd only had time to say hello when they arrived; his priority was Olivia and making sure she was comfortable. Now it was time to talk to his friend.

He found Shane in his study with Conor and Drew. Shane dropped his drink on the table and pulled Declan into a hug, slapping him twice on the back before he stepped back.

"It's been a long time, Deck," Shane said. "Too long."

Declan laughed. "In my defense, I've been on the run for eighteen months. It's a little hard to visit old friends when the cops are looking for you."

"Yeah, I had a couple of visits from the Feds asking about you. It was easy to say I hadn't seen you when I

Chapter 26

literally *hadn't* seen you in two years." Shane picked up his drink and took a drink. "And now you want my help."

"I didn't know who else to turn to, Shane," Declan said. "You're the only person I trust to help me with this. You don't have loyalty to either the Muldoon or O'Reilly family."

Shane Kelly was a lone wolf in the mob underground, a mercenary for hire. His loyalty belonged to whoever could pay him the most money. He had few friends in the world; luckily for Declan, he was one of them. Four years ago, two months before the Folger's Café shoot-out, Declan had saved Shane's life, pushing him out of the way of a car intent on running him down. Shane had sworn his undying loyalty to him on that day, promising to help Declan whenever he needed it.

"I need you, Shane," Declan said. "I can't do this alone. It's too big."

Shane nodded. "Anything for you, brother. Tell me what you want to do, and I will make it happen."

"I want to destroy Clyde Braniff. I want to make him regret being born. Can you help me do that?"

Shane downed the rest of his drink and slammed the glass on the desk. "With pleasure."

They spent the next hour working out a plan, one Declan thought might succeed. If this worked, Clyde Braniff would be out of his and Olivia's life forever.

After they wrapped things up, Conor and Shane headed to bed. Declan finished his drink and turned to leave.

"Are you sure about this, Deck?" Drew asked.

Drew had been quiet while he, Shane, and Conor made their plans. Declan intentionally left him out of them; he didn't want Drew to get hurt, so he would stay behind.

Declan nodded. "Yes, I'm sure."

Drew pinched the bridge of his nose. "What about Olivia? How do you think she's going to feel about this plan of yours?"

"She'll understand," Declan said. "I'm doing this for us." He cleared his throat. "I need you to take care of Liv, Drew. No matter what happens, you make sure she's safe."

"Stop talking like you're not coming back," Drew muttered.

"There's a chance I won't," Declan replied. He grabbed his empty glass and refilled it. He didn't want to think about not returning to Olivia, but he had to be realistic. In two swallows, he finished the whiskey.

Drew sighed. "Then you should stay here. Let Shane and Conor take care of this."

"No." Declan shook his head. "I need Clyde to see my face. He needs to understand that this is payback for what he did. It's essential that he grasps I am the one who destroyed his life, as he destroyed mine."

"What if he kills you?" Drew asked. "What then? Are you gonna let Liv lose you after she found you again? Do you really want to do that to her?" He leaned forward, his elbows on his knees. "Listen to me. This is your chance to walk away, to have a life with a woman you love. Don't throw it away for vengeance."

"I have no choice!" Declan yelled. He turned on his brother, his fists clenched, his ire rising. "I *have* to do this, Drew. Clyde took everything from me and destroyed my world. He did it because he could, because he was greedy and power-hungry. I will not let him take anything else from me."

"He could take your life," Drew whispered.

"He won't," Declan snapped.

Chapter 26

Shane stepped into the room behind Declan, arms crossed over his thick chest, his head tilted to one side.

"We good, brother?" he asked. He scratched his thick beard and stared at Drew.

"Yeah, we're good," Declan said. "Drew and I were just having a … disagreement. We're good now. Right, Drew?"

"Yeah," Drew said. "We're good."

Shane nodded and left quietly, without another word.

"I need to do this, Drew," Declan said. "And I need you to take care of my girl. Can you do that?"

Drew nodded, but he didn't speak.

"Promise me, Drew."

"I promise," his brother muttered.

That was all Declan needed. He went upstairs, leaving Drew in the study. Tonight, his plan was to sleep beside Olivia and hold her in his arms. He prayed it wouldn't be the last time.

Chapter 27
Olivia

Olivia remembered very little about the trip from the hospital. She didn't even know where they were. While in the car, the time she spent was in pain and semi-conscious, with her head on Declan's lap. She was a mess: weak, in pain, terrified, and plagued by nightmares. Pain clouded her mind in the brief moments when she gained consciousness.

She vaguely recalled arriving at a large mansion surrounded by an impenetrable brick wall. When the car stopped, Declan helped her out and carried her inside. Loud voices greeted them, and then someone mercifully put her in a soft bed. Declan convinced her to take a pain pill, and she sank into blissful oblivion.

When Olivia woke up, she was alone in a simple, yet elegant, bedroom. She sat up with minimal pain, then she got her feet under her and headed for the door. Stumbling a little, she reached for the pale blue silk robe draped over a chair. It surprised her to find that the door opened easily. She followed the hallway to a set of stairs, holding tight to the railing as she made her way to the bottom floor.

Olivia paused, heard voices, and followed them to a sunny dining room with a rectangular table.

Chapter 27

"Liv!" Declan shot out of his chair the second he laid eyes on her. He crossed the room, took her arm, and led her to a plush chair at the table. After helping her sit, he kneeled beside her with a concerned expression on his face. He rubbed her arm, his touch gentle.

"How are you?" he asked.

Olivia cupped his face and brushed her thumb across his cheekbone. "I'm okay," she whispered. "Where are we, Declan? Whose house is this?"

She heard someone clear their throat from the opposite side of the room. Declan rose to his feet, put his hand on her shoulder, and squeezed gently.

"Olivia, this is my friend, Shane Kelly," he said. "We're in his home in New Hampshire. Shane, this is Olivia Miller."

Shane smirked. "Miller? Really? Try again, brother. Remember, we don't keep secrets from each other. Especially with what we are about to do."

"Shane—."

Olivia put her hand on Declan's, silencing him. "Liv," she said. "My name is Liv O'Reilly." She narrowed her eyes. "But you already knew that, didn't you?"

Shane nodded. He got out of his chair and crossed the room to take her hand in his. He shook it, a soft smile on his face. "I think I like you, Liv O'Reilly. You're Sean O'Reilly's eldest daughter, right?"

Olivia nodded. "Yes, he's my father."

"Aw, yes, the wayward daughter. It's wonderful to meet you." Shane kissed her cheek, chuckled, and returned to his chair, clapping Declan on the shoulder as he passed him. He sat down and steepled his fingers under his chin. "Are you planning to go home to see your family, Ms. O'Reilly?"

Olivia made a face. "I would like to, but it hasn't been a possibility. Not right now."

"Perhaps that will change." Shane smiled. "Let's get you something to eat, shall we?"

His friendly words filled the air with a feeling of warmth. He had one of his men bring Olivia food and coffee before he returned to his discussion with Declan, Conor, and Drew.

Olivia sat back and enjoyed the first home-cooked meal she'd had in forever. She sipped the strong, sweet coffee, letting its warmth settle deep into her bones. Declan sat beside her, an arm over the back of her chair and his fingers resting on her shoulder.

"We should be back in three, maybe four days at the most," Shane said. "If everything goes according to plan."

"Plan? What plan?" Olivia asked. She turned to Declan. "Are you leaving?"

Declan nodded.

"Where are you going? Wherever it is, I'm going with you," Olivia said.

Shane chuckled. "You're not going anywhere, sugar. You are staying right here where you'll be safe and sound. We'll be back before you know it."

Olivia turned to Declan, her look questioning without saying a word. Declan cleared his throat and stood up.

"Will you excuse us? I think Liv and I need to talk." Declan took her arm, helped her to her feet, and led her out of the room.

They walked down a wide, grand hallway and into a small sitting room under the enormous staircase. Declan took her inside, closed the door behind them, and guided her to a loveseat in the corner. He helped her sit down before he perched on the edge of the couch beside her.

Chapter 27

"What is going on, Declan?" Olivia asked. She hated the way her voice shook as she spoke. "Where are you going?"

"We're going back to Boston," Declan replied. He refused to look into her eyes; instead, he gazed at her, their hands clenched together.

"Wh-what?" A scream rose in her throat, but she shoved it down. She concentrated on taking deep breaths, anything to calm her racing pulse and stop the panic building deep in her gut, trying to burst out of her in a primal scream. "Why? Why would you go back?"

"I have to go, sweetheart," Declan whispered. "If I don't do this, you will never be safe."

"Do what? What are you going to do?"

"We're going to take care of Clyde," he said. "Once and for all. I'm going to take care of him, and you will never have to worry again. You will be safe."

Olivia was on the verge of losing control. Tears fell from her eyes, her hands shook, and her stomach churned. Every fiber of her being screamed at her not to let him go. She gasped, unable to fill her lungs with air.

"Declan," she murmured. "Please, don't go. You want to keep me safe, but what about *you*? I need you safe and here with me. I know you think you need to kill Clyde, to make some grand gesture so he'll never bother us again, but I'm begging you not to go. For the love of God, Declan, do not go."

"I have to," he said. "I have no choice."

He took her chin in his hand, tilted her head back, and kissed her. It felt like a goodbye, and it made her heart ache. Declan brushed a tear from her cheek with his thumb and kissed the corner of her mouth.

"You stay here with Drew," he said. It was an order, his tone showing there was no room for argument. "He will take care of you until I get back. I promise you I *will* be back." He kissed her forehead. "I promise."

Declan walked out of the sitting room, leaving her alone. Olivia waited a few minutes before she followed, stepping into an empty hallway. She went up the stairs to the room they'd put her in and went straight to the window. From her vantage point, she could see the driveway. She watched Declan and Conor get into a car with Shane and drive away.

Olivia wiped at the tears rolling down her face. Dread settled in her heart. She would never see Declan again. He had finally come back to her, and she was going to lose him.

Once the car was out of sight, she turned away from the window and limped back to the bed. The pain from her injuries was awful, but not nearly as bad as the pain in her heart. She crawled into the bed, pulled the blankets over her head, and cried herself to sleep.

Chapter 28
Declan

"Do you think this is a good idea?" Conor asked as they watched the house across the street.

"No," Declan said. "But I don't think we have a choice."

Conor scratched his nose and looked at Declan out of the corner of his eye. "Are you going to tell Liv?"

"Eventually," Declan replied. "I think she'll understand why I did it and hopefully, it will mend the rift between her and her father."

"Or she'll get angry at you for that," Conor said with a snort. "I don't think any of us want to see Liv O'Reilly pissed off."

Declan chuckled. "I know I don't." He tapped Conor on the leg. "There's Shane."

Shane stopped at the corner, looked both ways, then he hurried across the street, yanked open the door, and climbed in the backseat.

"Sean said yes," Shane said. "If we need him, he will be there to help."

"How the hell did you manage that?" Declan asked.

"I told him what Clyde had Walsh do to Liv," Shane explained. "Then I told him what Clyde did to Olivia when she lived at the Muldoon compound. He was more than happy to cooperate." Shane checked his watch. "I'm scheduled to meet Muldoon in an hour. Apparently, he is staying at a safe house in Needham. He's been living there for almost two years."

Declan glanced at Shane in the rearview mirror. He loved his friend, but sometimes Shane scared him. His ability to get an audience with two of Boston's most influential and notorious mobsters was a testament to the unspoken power he wielded. His nonchalant attitude regarding what needed to be done to stop Clyde was even more frightening. He was soulless.

"What is it, Deck?" Shane asked.

"Nothing," Declan said. "I'm amazed at what you can do. And glad you're on my side."

"You should be," Shane said. "You don't want me as an enemy." Shane glowered at Declan for a moment before he burst out laughing. "Take me to Needham, driver."

Declan shook his head and laughed. "Anything for you, Shane."

Muldoon's safe house was a two-story Cape Cod in a quiet neighborhood in Needham. From the outside, no one would have guessed that one of Boston's most notorious mobsters was staying there. Unless you noticed the cameras outside the house or the men walking around every fifteen minutes.

From where Declan sat, the house appeared quiet, but appearances could be deceiving. Shane had gone in an hour earlier. Twenty minutes later, he sent one of his men out to get Conor. Declan was told to wait in the

Chapter 28

car. Shane refused to let him go inside until he spoke to Donovan Muldoon.

A black Escalade arrived fifteen minutes after Conor went inside. It parked across the street from Muldoon's temporary residence. The passenger side window rolled down, and Grady McCarthy stuck his head out.

Grady was Sean O'Reilly's second in command. Not a man to be reckoned with, that was for sure. Declan had been unlucky enough to have a run-in or two with the man when he was in his early twenties. One of those had been after Olivia had vanished from his life. It had been enough to chase away any ideas of rescuing Olivia from her cruel father that Declan might have had.

Back then, Grady was in his early thirties, ambitious and trying to make a name for himself with the O'Reilly family. Now he was in his mid-forties with prematurely gray hair and a neatly trimmed beard. Tattoos covered his arms, and he had a fierce countenance that terrified even the most hardened criminal. He had gained Sean O'Reilly's trust and positioned himself as his right-hand man. If he were here, Clyde Braniff would suffer.

"Good," Declan muttered to himself.

Declan hadn't wanted to involve Olivia's family, but Shane convinced him that Clyde left him no choice. Besides, it wouldn't hurt to have the O'Reillys on his side. Especially if he and Olivia planned to make a life together. Maybe this would prove to Sean O'Reilly that Declan deserved to be with Olivia.

The front door opened; Conor stepped out and gestured to Declan to come inside.

Declan checked his weapon, tucked it into the holster under his arm, got out of the car, and hurried up the stairs to the huge double doors leading inside. Just before he went in, he turned to look back at McCarthy. They held eye contact for a few seconds, then Grady nodded. Declan returned the nod, then he followed Conor inside.

They walked past the stairs and down a short hallway to a large wood paneled office at the back of the house. Conor stopped him with a hand to the chest before they entered.

"Are you sure about this, Deck?" Conor asked.

"Yeah, I'm sure," Declan replied. "You know as well as I do none of us are safe until we take care of Clyde. If Clyde somehow runs the Muldoon family, he will do everything in his power to destroy us. I won't let that happen." Declan put a hand on his friend's shoulder and squeezed. "Donovan needs to know what his nephew is up to, what he's trying to do. It's the only way to stop Clyde."

"God, I hope you're right." Conor shifted uneasily and stared at a spot above his friend's head. "If it means no more running, then I'm all for it. Especially if it means Ruthie will be safe."

"You're in love with that firecracker, aren't you?" Declan asked.

Conor chuckled. "Yeah, I think I am." He dropped his voice to a whisper. "What are you going to do if Donovan kills Clyde? Are you cool with that?"

"Clyde killed my sister, held my brother hostage for more than a year, and sent his goon to kill Olivia. As far as I'm concerned, death is too good for Clyde Braniff." Declan glanced at the closed office door. "Let's do this."

They stepped into the room. Donovan Muldoon sat behind a large desk against one wall while Shane sat across from him in a small, gray velvet chair. Muldoon rose to his feet as soon as Declan entered.

Chapter 28

"Declan, it's good to see you, boy. It's been a long time." He gestured to the chair beside Shane. "Won't you have a seat?"

Declan sat down while Conor stood right behind him. Donovan came out from behind the desk to perch on the front of it, directly in front of Shane and Declan.

"I understand you have some reliable information regarding my nephew," Muldoon said. "I'd like to hear it."

Declan cleared his throat. "Clyde was going to start a war with the O'Reillys."

Donovan shrugged. "Every day is a war with the O'Reillys. It's a fact of life."

"Not this time," Declan said. "He wanted me and my crew to steal a shipment of drugs and money from O'Reilly. His plan was to use the money to take over the family and remove you. He said he was sick of being under your thumb, following your rules, and being beholden to you."

"But he's my heir," Muldoon said. "It would have been his, eventually."

"I don't think he's willing to wait, Donovan," Declan said. "All Clyde cares about is the money and the power. Jesus Christ, do you know how much money I have made for that man in the last eighteen months?"

"What do you mean? How have you made him money?" Donovan interrupted. "I thought you got out, retired. After your sister died and your brother skipped town, Clyde said you moved to Maine somewhere because you didn't want to be part of the family anymore."

Declan scrubbed a hand over his face. "You don't know, do you?"

"Know what?" Donovan asked. "What the hell are you talking about?"

Shane leaned forward in his chair, his elbows on his knees. "Listen carefully, Mr. Muldoon. I'm going to be as succinct as possible. Clyde forced Declan to work for him, robbing banks up and down the coast. He did this by killing Declan's sister and holding his brother hostage."

Donovan sagged, and the breath left his lungs. He stared at Declan and shook his head. "I didn't ... I didn't know."

Declan sighed. "You have to understand, Mr. Muldoon. It was never enough. No matter how much money I stole for Clyde, it was never enough. He will risk a war between the families to get more. Clyde will kill Sean O'Reilly's daughter if it meant more money. Is that really the man you want as your heir?"

Donovan's face hardened, and a low growl came from his throat. He pointed at the man by the door. "Go get my nephew. I want a word with him."

The man hurried from the room. Donovan returned to the chair behind the desk, grimacing as he sat down.

"I need you to understand something," Donovan said. "My wife died giving birth to my son. The boy died when he was three days old. I never remarried; I never wanted to. My sister's son became my heir by default. I thought it was what he wanted. I didn't know he was unhappy. Obviously, I did *not* know what he was doing behind my back. I will not fight him to keep control of the family. I don't have the energy. But I sure the hell won't give it to him outright. The ungrateful, little bastard."

He stared at the men sitting in front of him, the sadness in his eyes obvious. Something was wrong, something more than an heir that didn't care about his family.

"What's wrong, Donovan?" Declan asked. "What is it?"

Chapter 28

Donovan smiled, but it didn't reach his eyes. "I'm dying, Declan. Lung cancer. My doctors say I have two, maybe three, months left to live."

The door opened, and Clyde entered with Donovan's man right on his heels. He froze as soon as he saw Declan.

"What the hell is this?" Clyde asked. "What are they doing here?"

"Have a seat, Clyde," Donovan said.

"Not until you tell me what's going on," Clyde snapped.

The man behind Clyde grabbed his shoulder, pushed him across the room, and forced him to sit on a small, wooden chair next to Donovan's desk.

Clyde's eyes darted around the room. They finally landed on his uncle, and he swallowed. "Uncle Donovan?"

"I understand you've been working on a change in leadership, nephew," Donovan said.

Clyde looked at Declan, then back at his uncle. "Wh-what? I don't understand."

"You heard me," Donovan said. "Do you want me out?"

Clyde visibly swallowed and clenched his hands in his lap. "Maybe."

Donovan crossed his arms over his chest and glared at his nephew. "It's a yes or no question, Clyde. Answer it."

Clyde sighed. "Yes, Uncle, I want you out."

Donovan rolled his eyes. "Why?"

Clyde snorted. "Why?" He leaned forward, the fear in his eyes replaced with hatred. "Because I *hate* you. I hate everything about you and this family. The honor system, the loyalty to a fake family, the inability to make a name for yourself outside of the damn family. The archaic rules you follow because of tradition. It's outdated, and frankly, it's a joke. You're a joke."

Donovan was out of his chair so fast he was nothing more than a blur. The crack of the slap Donovan planted on Clyde's face echoed through the room. He leaned over his nephew, so close that spittle hit Clyde in the face when Donovan spoke.

"You're out." He looked at Declan, Conor, and Shane, then he tipped his chin at the man standing behind the chair. "Step outside, Liam. I think these gentlemen would like a few minutes alone with my nephew."

Donovan followed Liam to the door. Just before he stepped out, he turned to look at Declan. "Declan, could I speak to you for a moment? Alone?"

Declan nodded, rose to his feet, and followed Donovan Muldoon out the door.

Chapter 29
Declan

When Declan returned to Donovan's office, Clyde was in a chair in the center of the room. Blood dripped from his nose and covered his upper lip, and he had a swollen eye that was shut. Shane stood in front of him with bruised, battered, bloody knuckles and a grin on his face. He stepped aside when Declan walked in, allowing Declan to stand in front of the mobster.

Declan stared at Clyde, the urge to kill the man overwhelming him. He reared back and hit Clyde as hard as he could. Clyde's head snapped around so hard, he fell out of the chair. He hit the floor with a sickening, yet satisfying, thump.

Clyde pushed himself to his knees, and to Declan's surprise, he laughed. "What's the matter, Deck? Are you upset about your girlfriend?" He shook his head as the laughter rumbled through his chest, echoing in Declan's ears. "You know, I would have given *anything* to see your face as Walsh cut into Olivia and made her bleed. I bet it was almost as good as when you found Sarah in that box. Too bad Walsh didn't finish the job like I did with Sarah."

Shane hauled Clyde to his feet and dropped him back on the chair. He leaned over the smaller man, his hands on the back of the chair on either side of Clyde's head. "Close your mouth," he said.

Declan shoved Shane out of the way, reared back, and hit Clyde hard enough to make his knuckles bleed. He lost count of the number of blows he landed. Clyde's left eye swelled shut, his lip split, blood flowed from both nostrils, and a deep cut appeared beneath one eye.

Declan could have gone on hitting him forever, anything to wipe the smug grin off his fucking face. But Declan didn't want him dead. Not yet anyway.

Declan took a step back and sucked in a giant lungful of air. "I'm done here," he muttered. He nodded at Conor. "Go get him." He waited until Conor was out the door, then he turned back to Clyde.

"I could kill you myself," Declan said. He closed his eyes and took a few deep breaths, calming himself. "Trust me, I *want* to kill you myself. But I think it would be better if you suffered. Like you made me suffer for more than a year. Like you made my sister suffer and Drew suffer. So, I asked your uncle if I could bring in someone to help me. He was very accommodating."

The door opened, and Donovan Muldoon entered. Right behind him was Grady McCarthy. Sheer terror dawned in Clyde's eyes as Sean O'Reilly's second-in-command stopped in front of him and smiled.

"Clyde, I'm sure you know Mr. McCarthy," Declan said. "He knows everything. In particular, he knows what you did to O'Reilly's daughter."

"Mr. O'Reilly also knows what you did to his daughter," Grady said. He crouched in front of Clyde and stared up at him. "Not that I need it, but I have his permission to do whatever I want to you."

Chapter 29

"He has mine as well," Donovan said. "I'm finished with you, Clyde."

"My mother—." Clyde gagged and blood dribbled from his mouth.

Donovan shook his head. "I'll handle my sister," he said. He turned to Declan. "Once Liv is feeling up to it, you come see me. I'll have everything ready. Grady, take care of this scum and get him out of my house."

Declan gave Clyde one last look as he shook first Donovan's hand, then Grady's. Then he followed Conor and Shane out the door. He didn't turn back, even when he heard the first scream of pain.

Notorious Boston Mobster Found Dead in Boston Harbor.
Declan knew the details, so he only half-listened to the newsflash on the radio. They had found Clyde Braniff floating in Boston Harbor. When they pulled him from the water, it was obvious that someone tortured him, as bruises and cuts covered almost every inch of his body. The police had no suspects.

As much as Declan wanted to celebrate the death of the man who killed his sister, held his brother captive, and raped the woman he loved, he couldn't. Not until he had Olivia safely back in his arms.

"Did you call the mansion?" Declan asked.

Shane nodded. "They know we're on our way back. James assured me he would give the message to Ms. O'Reilly himself. He also said it will thrill her to see you."

James wasn't lying. Olivia stood in the driveway when they pulled in. He wasn't even out of the car before she flung herself into his arms and pressed kisses to his neck and face.

Declan held her tight and breathed her in. Even though it had only been three days, it had been too long. Every second away from Olivia was a second too long.

Declan hugged her close, sighing into her mouth as he returned her kiss. "God, I missed you," he whispered when they broke apart.

"I missed you too," she said. "Why didn't you answer my texts or calls?"

"I'm afraid that's my doing, love," Shane said, as he climbed from the car. "I have a strict no phone rule when I'm negotiating. Nothing messes it up more than someone's phone going off at a critical moment. But he's home now, safe and sound."

"Thank you, Shane," Olivia said.

Declan squeezed her hand. "I need to talk to you," he said. "It's important."

Olivia nodded. "Yeah, sure."

"Use my office," Shane said.

Declan held her hand tight as they walked inside and through the house to Shane's office. Declan ushered her inside and closed the door.

Olivia crossed her arms and stared at Declan. "What is it?"

"I don't think you're going to like it," he said.

She closed her eyes. "Then tell me and get it over with," she muttered.

"Donovan wants me to take over the Muldoon family."

"What?"

Declan sat on the sofa against the wall. "Donovan Muldoon is dying, Liv. Clyde was his heir—."

"But now Clyde is dead," Olivia interrupted.

Chapter 29

"Exactly. Donovan and I were close once, a long time ago, when my father and I both worked for him. He's old and dying, and he wants to leave his family, his birthright, in excellent hands. He said he always trusted me, believed in me. He doesn't have an heir, and he doesn't have a lot of time." Donovan patted the sofa beside him. "Come sit with me."

Olivia sat beside him, her feet tucked under her and her head on his shoulder. "What are you going to do?"

Declan kissed the top of her head. "I'm going to do it."

Olivia tipped her head back and looked at him. "What does that mean for us?"

He shrugged. "Well, I believe you were supposed to marry the Muldoon heir to unite the families and help bring peace, weren't you?"

Olivia narrowed her eyes, a faint smile dancing across her lips. "I believe I was, yes. But that was three years ago, and a lot has changed."

"So, you don't think your father will allow you to marry the heir to the Muldoon family anymore?" Declan asked.

"Well, there's only one way to find out," Olivia said. "I have to talk to my father."

Olivia squeezed Declan's hand so hard, her nails dug into the palm. She shifted in her seat, glanced at the door, then down at the menu on the table in front of her.

"Hey," Declan said. "Look at me."

Olivia looked up, her lower lip caught between her teeth, and her eyes wide and frightened.

"It's okay. Everything will be fine," he said.

Olivia grimaced. "You don't know my father, Declan. He's a hard man. And that's on a good day."

"Liv!"

A tall, blonde girl with an athletic build burst through the door of the café and raced toward their table. Olivia moved just as quickly, climbing to her feet to meet the girl halfway. They embraced, both crying.

"What are you doing here? I thought you were away at school," Olivia asked.

"When I found out Daddy was meeting you here, I had to come," the blonde explained. "God, I've missed you."

Olivia peered around the blonde. "Where's Daddy?"

"He's coming. Grady wouldn't let them out of the car until he checked things out. I didn't care." The girl rolled her eyes. "I'm sure I'll hear about it later."

Declan cleared his throat. Olivia swung around, a blush coloring her cheeks.

"Shit, sorry," Olivia said. "Declan, this is my little sister, Caitlin. Caitlin, this is Declan Quinn."

Declan rose to his feet and held out his hand. "Nice to meet you, Caitlin."

Caitlin looked him up and down as she shook his hand. "Handsome, Liv. Nice job."

Olivia punched her sister on the shoulder and giggled. They both sat down, and Declan couldn't help but notice how alike the sisters were. They didn't look alike; Caitlin was tall, blonde, thin, and athletic, while Olivia was a few inches shorter than Caitlin, with dark hair and a more voluptuous body. Their mannerisms gave them away—the identical laughter, the way they sat, and the way they spoke.

Out of the corner of his eye, Declan saw Grady McCarthy stalk through the café door. He stopped as the

Chapter 29

door swung closed and looked around. Once he saw the sisters, he opened the door and held it open.

Sean O'Reilly entered. No one looked in his direction, not because they didn't know he was there, but because they were keenly aware of his presence. No one looked at him because they didn't want to draw his attention or his ire.

A gorgeous, regal woman followed O'Reilly through the door. As soon as she saw Liv and Caitlin, she pushed past O'Reilly and rushed across the room.

"Olivia!" she cried.

"Mom!"

The family reunion went on for several minutes. Declan sat at the table, out of the way, with no intention of disturbing Olivia's joyous return to the O'Reilly family. He didn't move until Sean O'Reilly reached out to shake his hand.

"Thank you for bringing my daughter home, Mr. Quinn."

Declan jumped to his feet and shook the mobster's hand. "My pleasure, sir."

"Let's have a seat," he said. "I understand they have made some changes in the Muldoon family hierarchy, and we need to talk."

"Yes, sir, you are correct." Declan cleared his throat. "We need to talk."

Chapter 30

Olivia

An hour after her parents and sister arrived, Declan and her father moved to the other side of the restaurant. Olivia knew they were talking about the recent changes to the Muldoon hierarchy and, most likely, her. She itched to get out of her seat and join them; after all, they were discussing *her* life. But she knew her father wouldn't approve, and it might stop any negotiations. She would wait and join them when the time was right.

That time came close to midnight. Grady approached the table where she sat with her mother and sister.

"Excuse me, Ms. O'Reilly?" Grady said. "Your father would like to speak to you."

Caitlin glanced at Grady and made a face, but before she could say anything, Olivia was on her feet and thanking Grady for his help. She made her way across the restaurant to the booth where her father and Declan waited. Olivia sat down beside Declan.

"Daddy," Olivia murmured. "You wanted to speak to me?"

Sean O'Reilly nodded. "Before we go any further, I want to apologize to you."

Chapter 30

Her father never apologized, ever. Olivia stared at him. "You want to apologize? For what?"

O'Reilly scrubbed a hand over his face. "It was stupid of me to expect you to marry someone you didn't know in order to unite our families. It was an old-fashioned, archaic idea that I should have rejected from the beginning. I was so desperate to avoid a war between the families. So, I forced my daughter into a marriage she didn't want to save face. I should have told Donovan Muldoon I wasn't interested as soon as he broached the subject. I'm sorry I let it go as far as it did." He reached across the table and grasped her hands. "I'm sorry you got hurt. If I had known—."

"It's okay," Olivia whispered.

O'Reilly shook his head. "No, it's not. If I could kill Clyde Braniff again, I would. Luckily, Declan took care of that for me. I am extremely grateful to him." He cleared his throat. "I understand the two of you have a ... special relationship? Is that right?"

Olivia nodded. "Yes, sir."

"Declan's a good man, Liv. I'm sorry I didn't see it sooner." Her father squeezed her hands. "Whatever you decide to do, I will support you. Your life is your own, Liv, and I will respect your decisions."

"Thank you, Daddy," Olivia said. "I appreciate that."

"Yes, thank you, Mr. O'Reilly," Declan added. "I promise to take good care of her."

"I know you will." O'Reilly smiled at her and Declan, then he rose to his feet. "What do you say we get out of here so they can close this place up?"

After seeing her family for the first time in three years, Olivia was emotionally exhausted. She fell into bed as soon as they stepped into the bedroom. Her face hit the pillow, and she was asleep.

Olivia woke up several hours later to an empty bed. She crawled out, grabbed Declan's shirt from the chair where he'd thrown it, put it on, and buttoned it to the top of the swell of her breasts. She went into the bathroom where she brushed her teeth, washed her face, and ran a comb through her long hair. When she came out of the bathroom, Declan was on the bed, sitting against the headboard with his arms crossed, watching TV.

"Hi," Olivia said.

"Hey," he said. "Why don't you come sit with me?" He patted the bed.

Declan watched Olivia as she crossed the room, climbed onto the bed, and crawled toward him. He caught his lower lip between his teeth, and a pink flush colored his cheeks. His eyes were wide, the green nearly swallowed by his lust-blown black pupils. As Olivia crawled toward him, his tongue snaked out of his mouth and licked his full, kissable lips.

A growl rumbled from his chest. "That's my shirt."

Olivia stopped and sat back on her heels. "Yeah, it is."

Declan launched himself down the bed, tackling Olivia and pulling her under him. He slid his hands beneath the T-shirt, his calloused fingers rough against her sensitive skin. His kiss was hard and possessive, and he sucked her tongue into his mouth. He cupped her breast, pinching and twisting the nipple until Olivia arched her back and moaned.

Heat pooled into the pit of her stomach as Declan kissed and caressed her. He ran his hand down her

Chapter 30

stomach and between her legs. He eased his fingers into her, crooking it to brush against her sweet spot, sending a shot of pure pleasure through her.

"Jesus, Declan," she gasped.

He grunted and fucked her with his fingers, the heel of his hand rubbing deliciously against her clit, making every inch of her body tremble. Declan kissed every inch of her neck, adding to the intense sensations overwhelming her.

Entranced by the way they moved, the sounds they made, and the pleasure they felt, the rest of the world melted away. The room smelled of both soap and sweat, and the couple's noises mixed with the sound of the TV's laughter.

Olivia wanted him just as much, if not more, than she usually did. She wanted his hands on her, his mouth on hers, inside her, filling her, taking her, and making her his. She craved the intimate connection achieved through the merging of their bodies, a connection she only seemed to have with Declan. Time and space became irrelevant to her. The only thing her body could focus on was the climax exploding through her.

Declan released her long enough to pull her underwear off. Leaning over her, he kissed her inner thigh and pushed up her shirt beneath her breasts. He stretched out on the bed, his head between her legs, his mouth on her pussy, his tongue lapping at the wetness pooling between her legs. He sucked her clit into his mouth and rolled his tongue over it, sending a shot of intense pleasure blasting through her.

Olivia relaxed against the bed and let Declan take over. He shifted, his upper body sliding up the bed as he pulled himself closer so he could bury his tongue inside her. Olivia's hips rocked as she rode his tongue, her body writhing in ecstasy, faint gasps of pleasure leaving her. She was so close, though it didn't surprise her. Declan seemed to have that effect on her, easily bringing her to orgasm every time they were together.

Olivia's entire body shook from the orgasm raging through her, every nerve ending on fire, explosions of white light going off behind her closed eyes. She squeezed her thighs together and tangled her fingers in Declan's hair, holding him against her.

Declan was insatiable. His grip tightened on her even as she came, quiet grunts coming from him as he continued licking and sucking, keeping her on edge and pulling multiple orgasms from her.

He held her until the trembling passed, and she could take a deep breath. Only then did he stand up, shuck off his clothes, and pull her to the end of the bed and into his arms. Olivia was on her knees at the end of the bed in front of him. Declan unbuttoned the shirt she wore and pushed it off. Once she was naked, he turned her around, his chest pressed to her back, covering her in kisses. He caressed her, his hand moving down her stomach to her sex. He slipped his fingers into her and pumped them in and out, intentionally brushing them over that spot that made sparks flit across her skin.

Declan rubbed his cock against her, groaning against her neck. Olivia dug her nails into his arms as she ground down on his fingers, and he rutted against her. He pushed her onto her stomach, his knees on either side of hers, and entered her from behind with one hard thrust.

She pushed back against him, groaning, her fingers twisted in the blankets of the bed, holding tight as Declan slammed into her. His hips shot forward, so he buried his

Chapter 30

cock deep inside her as he fucked her at an erratic pace. He growled her name, and his body tensed as he came.

Olivia collapsed face-first onto the bed, Declan on top of her, both struggling to catch their breath. Declan's rough hands caressed her back. Every few seconds, he pressed a soft kiss to her shoulder or neck. After a few minutes, he grabbed a blanket from the end of the bed and pulled it over them.

"Tell me what happened," Olivia whispered, after she composed herself. "I need to know."

Declan shared what happened after he, Shane, and Conor left the mansion, starting slowly but eventually pouring out the complete story.

When he finished, Olivia kissed the corner of his mouth, then she laid her head on his chest. "I can't believe it's over," she said.

"You're safe. That's all that matters." He twirled a strand of her hair around his fingers. "You're free. You can go anywhere you want and do anything you want."

Olivia tipped her head back to look at him. "You know that's not what I want. The only thing I want, Declan Quinn, is to stay right here with you. I'm not going anywhere. We're in this together."

Declan arched an eyebrow. "For better or for worse?"

"Is that a proposal, Mr. Quinn?"

Declan chuckled. "Yeah, I guess it is." He rested his forehead against hers. "You think you can handle being married to the head of the Muldoon family?"

"I think I can handle that," Olivia said. "But we're doing this together, me and you. Partners. Deal?"

"Deal." A smile spread across Declan's face. "I love you, Olivia O'Reilly."

"I love you too, Declan Quinn."

The End

Book Club Questions

1. Declan and Olivia hadn't seen each other in eight years. Do you think it's possible that Declan wouldn't recognize Olivia after not seeing her for so long? Have you ever seen someone after a long time and not recognized them at first?
2. Did Declan make the right choice working for Clyde to save his family? Why or why not?
3. Olivia tried to do the right thing for her family by marrying Clyde. Do you think she should have looked out for herself instead?
4. How important was family to the characters in *Taken by the Mobster*?
5. Did you find Olivia to be manipulative?
6. Do you think Declan should have blown up the mansion after rescuing Olivia from the Muldoon compound? Why or why not?
7. Olivia had the chance to ask Officer Willet for help. Do you think Olivia should have let her help?
8. What is your opinion of Declan taking over the Muldoon family?

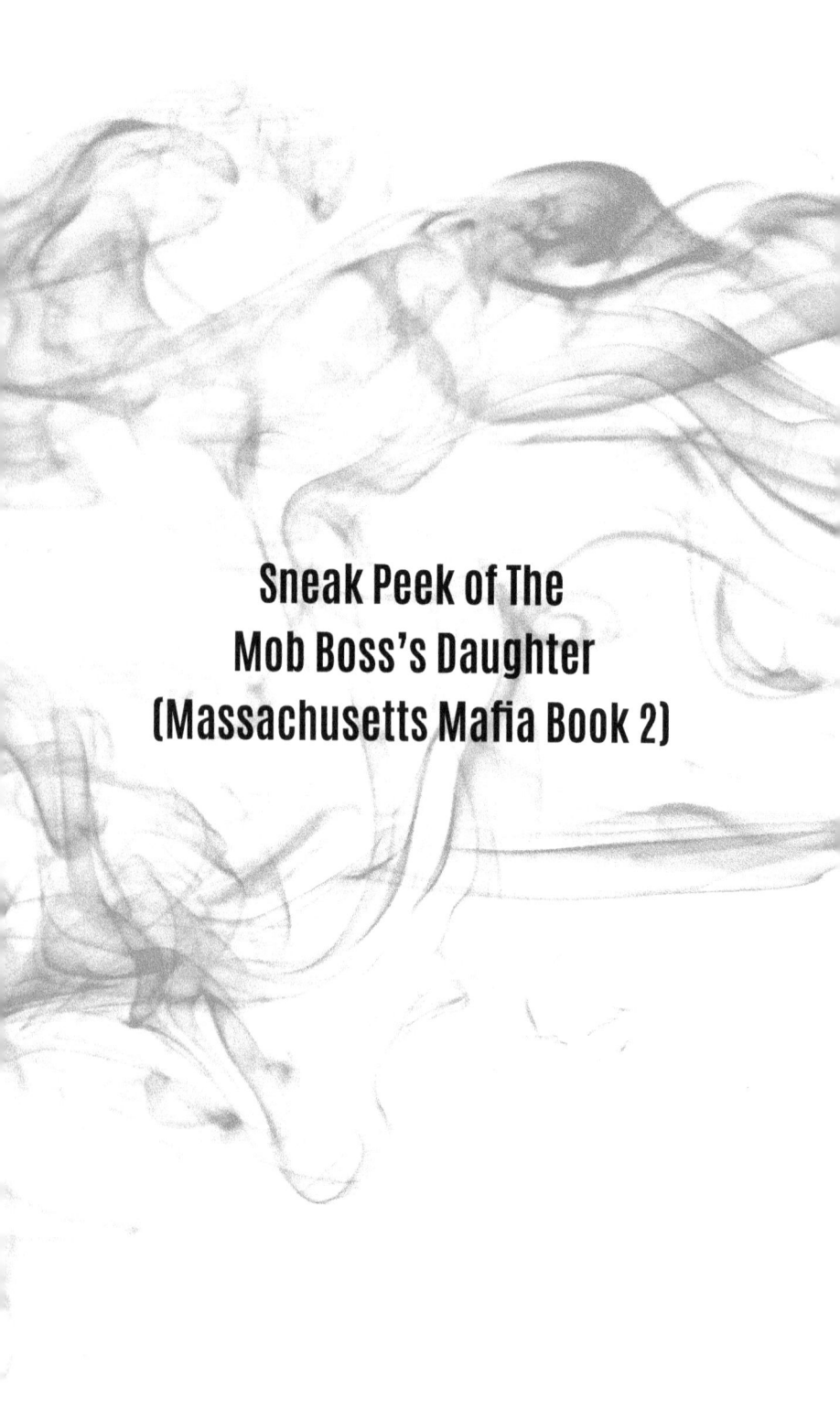

Sneak Peek of The Mob Boss's Daughter (Massachusetts Mafia Book 2)

Chapter 1
Caitlin

"I think I had too much to drink." Caitlin giggled, as she tried to put her key in the lock for the third time. She couldn't get it to line up; it kept hitting the edge and bouncing away.

Bobby plucked her keys out of her hands. "Let me try." He closed one eye and pointed the key at the door. After three attempts, he finally got it in the keyhole, turned it, and shoved open the door.

"God, I hope it's not that hard to get it in later." He burst out laughing and winked at Caitlin.

She punched him on the shoulder. "Funny. I hope you're not serious." She went into the small kitchen, tossed her purse on the table, and opened the cupboard next to the fridge. "I gotta feed the cat."

Bobby groaned. "Not that stupid cat. It isn't even yours."

"If I don't feed it, who will?" Caitlin opened the can of cat food and dumped it in a plastic dish. "It's only going to take me a minute."

"Whatever." Bobby shucked off his jacket and sat on the couch. "Just hurry."

He didn't see the dirty look Caitlin gave him. She opened the living room window, set the food outside on the fire escape, and stuck her head out.

"Here kitty, kitty," she called.

Where is that dumb cat?

Caitlin glanced at Bobby over her shoulder. He was half asleep on her couch, feet propped on the coffee table, hands folded on his stomach. He could wait; this wouldn't take long. She ducked her head and climbed out the window onto the fire escape.

"Kitty?" She looked over the edge of the fire escape and sure enough, there it was, two stories down. When she called it again, it bounded up the fire escape and landed right in front of her. It rubbed against her legs and purred.

"Hi there, kitty," Caitlin whispered, as she crouched down to pet it.

At first, she didn't understand what she was hearing; a loud boom and then voices coming from her apartment. She heard Bobby shout, then a grunt, followed by things crashing to the floor.

"Listen, you little bastard," she heard someone say. "Where the fuck is it?"

"I don't know what the hell you're talking about," Bobby muttered. "I swear to God."

Caitlin plastered herself against the wall outside the window and peered around the corner. Two men stood in the middle of her living room with their backs to the window. Bobby sat on the floor with his hand pressed to his nose and blood seeping through his fingers.

"Where's your girlfriend, Bobby boy?" one man asked.

"Joey, listen—."

"Where is she?" Joey asked again.

Chapter 1

Bobby's eyes darted to the window, then back. "Not here. She went out for cat food."

Joey spoke while the other man took a gun from his pocket and pointed it at Bobby's head. "You better start talking," Joey said. "Mr. Moretti is not happy. You stole something that belongs to him, and he wants it back. I am only going to ask you once. What did you do with the E and the Special K?"

Bobby wiped his nose with the back of his hand. "Okay, Joey, okay. I ... I sold it."

"You better be fucking joking," the man with the gun said.

Bobby shook his head. "God, I wish I was." He took a deep breath. "Look, I'm sorry. I needed cash, and I figured I could get it back."

Joey laughed. "How the fuck did you think you were gonna get back a hundred grand worth of drugs?"

Bobby's eyes widened, and Caitlin heard genuine panic in his voice when he spoke. "A hundred grand? Did you say a hundred grand?"

"Yes, you little dipshit," the other guy said. "It was a hundred grand worth of dope. How much did you sell it for?"

"Twenty," Bobby whispered.

"Fucking idiot," Joey said. He shook his head. "Take care of him, Gino. I want to get out of here before the girl comes back."

Gino stepped closer to Bobby and pressed the gun to the center of his forehead. Caitlin jumped back, her hand going to her mouth to stifle her scream when the gun went off. Tears leaked from her eyes.

Oh, my God. Oh, my God.

Caitlin stayed outside, pressed against the wall. She couldn't hear anything over the pounding in her ears. The urge to move overwhelmed her. She took a chance, crept to the window, and peered in.

Her living room looked like a slaughterhouse. Blood covered every surface–floor, couch, coffee table, the wall. Brain matter covered her blue-and-white rug, a gift from her mother.

Caitlin gasped as her stomach turned, and her gorge rose. She gnawed on her lower lip and prayed she wouldn't vomit.

"Did you hear that?" a voice said from her bedroom.

She moved away from the window, her eyes darting around, her hand on her mouth.

Fuck. They heard me.

The cat sauntered past her and down the fire escape. She looked over the edge, then back at the window. She could hear the men moving through her apartment, heading her way. Staying here would get her killed. Decision made, she grabbed the railing and started down the ladder. Just as she got to the floor below hers, she heard men shouting above her.

Caitlin ran down the New York streets, jumping at every shadow, fear forcing her to move as quickly as possible. For the first time in her twenty-two years on this earth, she wished she had a gun. Maybe she should have taken Grady up on one of his ten thousand offers to teach her to use a weapon.

After twenty blocks, her legs felt like rubber and her lungs burned, so she slowed to a stop. She turned in a

Chapter 1

circle, trying to get her bearings. On the corner across the street, she saw Katz's Delicatessen, so she crossed against the light and ducked inside.

An irritated young man behind the counter served her coffee, then she found a table facing the door. She eased into her seat and took her phone from her back pocket.

Caitlin hesitated, unsure whether she should call the police or call her father. While her father was a powerful man in Boston, he had no pull in New York City. She had heard him speaking of the Boston and New York crime families' lack of respect and communication multiple times.

If she called the police, they would want answers. Why had she run? What was Bobby into? Did she know the men who killed him? Caitlin couldn't give them the answers they would want.

That left only one option.

Her hand shook as she pulled up his number on her phone. She exhaled and hit the button.

Three hours. Caitlin didn't know if she could wait that long. Fortunately, she kept her credit card in her phone case, since she'd run out of the apartment with nothing. If she kept ordering coffee, she'd be able to stay in the deli until Grady arrived. After she finished the first cup, she returned to the counter, grabbed two magazines, and ordered more coffee and a sandwich. The irritated young man behind the counter didn't even look at her as he rang her up and handed Caitlin her food.

Thank God Grady answered when she called; Caitlin knew he would. Her father would not be happy if he found out that Grady did not answer a call from one of the O'Reilly daughters.

Not that Liv would call; she had Declan. He would protect Caitlin's sister with his life.

Caitlin shifted in her chair to keep her ass from falling asleep. Her mind wouldn't stop replaying the sound of the bullet tearing through Bobby's forehead and the loud *thunk* his body made when it hit the floor. Just thinking about it made her want to puke.

She forced herself to quit thinking about it. Instead, she tried to picture Grady driving to her rescue. She would never say it out loud to anyone, but she'd had a huge crush on Grady for the last two years. It wasn't like she could help it; the man was always around, always right there in her face. He was at every family gathering, he hung around their house all the time, and he went everywhere the family went. Caitlin couldn't get rid of Grady if she wanted to.

Not that she wanted to. He was easy on the eyes and so damn attractive with his salt-and-pepper hair and neatly trimmed beard. He was well built, too. Huge biceps, one of which had a tattoo, rumored to be the McCarthy family crest, though no one knew for sure. Then there was the six-pack abdomen and the chest ready to burst from the too tight T-shirts he favored. He also had an ass you could bounce a quarter off. The man was a walking GQ ad, and he didn't even know it.

The only thing marring his perfect looks was the perpetual scowl he wore on his face. Caitlin never saw him smile. He was all business and insanely devoted to her father. Grady McCarthy's only mission in life was to do as Sean O'Reilly commanded.

Chapter 1

Caitlin knew nothing would ever come of her crush on Grady. The man was twenty-two years older than her, and her father's *dara i gceannas*—second-in-command. Any relationship between them had to remain platonic. Anything else would be a scandal, taboo, and irresponsible. That didn't stop Caitlin from fantasizing about Grady every chance she got.

Exhaustion washed over her. Caitlin rested her head on the wall behind her and closed her eyes. She tried to calm her racing heart and overactive brain by taking several deep, cleansing breaths.

It must have worked because the next thing she knew, the bell over the delicatessen door jingled, and Grady McCarthy strode through. He surveyed the restaurant, turning slowly until his eyes landed on Caitlin. Before he could say anything, she shot out of her seat and threw herself into his arms.

Caitlin buried her face against the side of his neck and inhaled the clean, manly scent that was all Grady McCarthy—soap and Old Spice deodorant and cologne. She could have stayed there forever, but Grady grabbed her and held her at arm's length.

"What the hell is going on, Caitlin?" he asked. "Explain to me why I had to drive three hours to rescue you. And it better be good."

"It's not good, Grady. It's bad. Really, *really* bad."

Chapter 2
Grady

Grady shoved the naked girl away from him and reached for his ringing phone. Swearing, he watched it fall to the floor. He threw the blankets off, dropped to his knees, and snatched it from under the bed. He sat on the floor, naked, with his head resting on the edge of the bed.

"Yeah," he muttered.

"Grady? Is that you?"

"Who is this?" he asked.

"It's Caitlin." The girl on the phone dragged in a shaky breath. "I … I need your help."

Grady pushed himself to his feet, sat on the bed, and checked his watch. "Fuck, Caitlin, it's one in the morning. This better be good. What happened?"

Knowing Caitlin, the possibilities were endless: drunk, high, another car accident, boy problems, or maybe she'd ended up in Canada again.

"I'm in trouble." Her voice dropped to a whisper. "Grady, I'm in big trouble, and I'm scared. I need your help."

Caitlin O'Reilly was the youngest daughter of Grady's boss, Sean O'Reilly, head of the O'Reilly crime family in Boston. If she needed him, he would go without hesitation, no questions asked. Part of his responsibilities as

Chapter 2

Sean's second-in-command was to take care of the family. All of them. Even if they drove him crazy like Caitlin did.

He held his phone against his shoulder, snatched his pants off the floor, and put them on, no underwear in sight. "Tell me where you are."

"I'm at Katz's Delicatessen near NYU," she whispered.

"Go home. I'll meet you at your apartment. You can tell me what happened when I get there."

"I ... I can't go home." Caitlin's voice caught, and a sob escaped her. "It's not safe."

His patience was wearing thin. "What the fuck, Caitlin? I don't understand why it's not safe. What did you do?"

"Please, Grady. I can't explain over the phone. You'll have to see it; otherwise, you won't believe me. Can you come?"

He snatched his T-shirt and jacket from the chair and looked around the room for his shoes. "Listen to me, Caitlin. Stay where you are. If anything happens, call me. I'll get there as soon as I can." He ended the call and shoved his phone in his front pocket.

It was a three-hour drive to New York. He could take the jet, but by the time he got it fueled and filed the flight plans, he could drive it.

"Hey." He patted the girl in his bed on the ass. "Get up. Time to go."

The girl rolled over and squinted at him. "What?" she asked.

"I gotta go. Get out." Once he had his dark gray T-shirt on, he tucked his holstered gun into the waistband of his pants. "Now."

The girl—some young thing he'd picked up at the bar—climbed out of the bed with a huff and pulled on her clothes. She couldn't have been more than a year or two older than Caitlin. He liked them young, and, despite his age, they liked him.

After she dressed, Grady ushered the girl through the apartment to the front door.

She paused and took something from her purse. "Call me." She smiled and pushed a business card into his hand. "We'll get drinks."

Grady nodded. "Yeah, maybe." He opened the door and shoved her out, shutting it firmly behind her. The business card went in the trash. He wouldn't see her again.

Once he had his car keys and his wallet, he locked up the apartment and took the elevator down to the parking garage. Grady debated whether he should call Sean and tell him about Caitlin, but he quickly rejected the idea. If Caitlin called him before her father, there was a reason. He would find out what happened and fill Sean in later.

Grady climbed into his black Escalade, plugged in his phone, turned on some AC/DC, and pulled out of the garage. Traffic was light as he drove through Boston to the freeway. Once he pulled onto the I-90 East, he got in the left lane and set the cruise control to ninety. With any luck, he'd be in New York in less than three hours.

Grady found a parking spot right in front of the deli; no surprise at four in the morning. Inside, he stopped at the front of the store and looked around. He spotted Caitlin right away, but before he could do or say anything, she was on her feet and throwing herself into his arms.

Caitlin pressed her face against his neck, and her hair tickled his cheek. He resisted the urge to hug her close and kiss her temple.

Chapter 2

What the fuck? This is Caitlin, for Christ's sake. Get a grip, McCarthy.

He grabbed her upper arms and pushed her away, rougher than he intended, but he needed her to understand this was business.

"What the hell is going on, Caitlin? Explain to me why I had to drive for three hours to rescue you. And it better be good."

Caitlin looked at him with tears in the corner of her eyes. "It's not good, Grady. It's bad. Really, *really* bad."

Caitlin O'Reilly never cried. Not when her sister disappeared for three years, or when her father got shot at Folger's Café. The girl kept her emotions in check all the time. Something—or someone—had scared her.

Grady released her, took her hand, and guided her back to the table. He helped her into the chair, then sat down beside her.

"What happened?" he asked.

Caitlin swallowed and stared at her hands. Without looking at Grady, she explained what had happened. By the time she was done, Grady had his hands clenched in front of him and his head pounded.

He rubbed the center of his forehead. "Did they see you?"

"I ... I think so," she whispered. "I think they saw me when I was going down the fire escape. But maybe only my back or the top of my head."

Grady grabbed her chin and forced her to look at him. "This is important, Cait. Think. Did they see you?"

Caitlin caught her lip between her teeth and shrugged. "I don't know."

Grady released her and stood up. "We need to go to your place."

She shook her head. "I don't want to."

"You can wait in the car while I check out the apartment," Grady explained. "Let's go."

Caitlin didn't utter a word on the drive to her apartment, which was unlike her. Normally, she talked his ear off, spouting off about topics he didn't give a shit about. He didn't like this version of Caitlin.

"You have your phone, right?" Grady said, after he parked down the street from her apartment building.

Caitlin nodded but didn't speak.

"I'm going inside. Call me if you see anything strange."

Caitlin didn't respond. She stared straight ahead.

"Damn it, Caitlin, look at me."

"What?" she snapped. She rolled her hazel eyes, flipped her hair off her shoulder, and crossed her arms.

There she was. That was the Caitlin he knew, pissed off at the world and everyone in it, especially anyone who worked for her father.

Grady grabbed the door handle. "I will be right back. I'm going to check your apartment."

Caitlin sighed. "I locked the door, and my keys are inside. You can't get in."

He reached past her, his hand brushing her leg as he opened the glove compartment and pulled out a key on a small green key ring. He shook it in her face.

"I can get in," Grady said.

Her eyes narrowed. "How did you get a key to my apartment?"

Now it was Grady's turn to roll his eyes. "Your father gave it to me. In case I needed it."

"Fuck my father," Caitlin muttered.

Grady grabbed her upper arm and dragged her close. "Watch your mouth, young lady. Have some respect."

Chapter 2

Caitlin snorted, yanked her arm out of his grasp, and turned away from him. She stared out the passenger window.

Grady cursed under his breath, shoved open the door, and headed for the apartment building. Caitlin was already on his nerves. He needed to figure out what the hell happened, get it straightened out, and get away from her. The last few times he'd been around her, he'd felt off. Caitlin usually irritated him, but recently he'd noticed she had grown into a beautiful, confident woman. He didn't dare admit it, even to himself, but he found Caitlin attractive. But she was his boss's daughter and, therefore, off-limits. She was one twenty-something he wouldn't be sleeping with.

He had only been to Caitlin's apartment once. Her sophomore year she had wrecked her car—for the third time—and he drove a new one to New York and delivered it to her.

Caitlin thought he came to New York to deliver her car, but, in reality, he had been making the trip anyway. He had a scheduled meeting with the Moretti family to discuss business. It was easy enough to drop off the car at Caitlin's apartment before meeting the New York version of Sean O'Reilly.

Grady unlocked the building's front door with the key and stepped inside. No elevator because Caitlin insisted on living close to campus in a no-frills apartment. She didn't flaunt her family's wealth and didn't want anyone to know she was a mob boss's daughter.

Caitlin lived on the sixth floor. Her place was at the end of a long hallway, the last door on the left. He looked over his shoulder back down the hallway before unlocking the door and stepping inside.

The smell of blood assaulted him as soon as he was inside. He could see Bobby's body from the door, the blood congealing beneath him. Grady took his gun from his waistband and stepped further into the apartment. It was dead quiet.

No one was in the apartment, not that he expected anyone to be there. He took his phone from his pocket and made a phone call. The person he spoke with assured him that within an hour, someone would be at Caitlin's apartment to take care of it.

In the kitchen, he found Caitlin's open purse on the table; the contents spilled everywhere. He pushed the items around, looking for her driver's license. It was gone.

Shit.

Grady tucked his gun back into the holster in his waistband and headed downstairs. He had just stepped onto the street when his phone rang.

"Yeah," he answered.

"Grady, they're here," Caitlin said.

"What? Who's here?" Grady asked.

"The guys who killed Bobby," she replied. "They're at the coffee shop. I think they're watching the building."

Grady picked up the pace and hurried down the sidewalk, sticking to the shadows, grateful that the sun wasn't up all the way. Less than fifty feet from where he'd parked the SUV, he saw a small coffee shop. Two men sat inside with paper cups of coffee and uneaten pastries in front of them. Neither of them looked like they belonged in a neighborhood filled with college students.

As he got closer, Grady realized he knew one man sitting at the table. Gaetano "Joey" LaGuardia worked for Frank Moretti as a *forneart*—enforcer. If Joey LaGuardia was here, that meant the Moretti family was involved.

Chapter 2

Everything changed at that moment. This wasn't some kid being stupid and screwing up a drug deal. This involved the New York mob, an entity Grady couldn't take on alone. If Moretti thought Caitlin knew anything, or that she might go to the police, he would do everything in his power to stop her.

Fuck. Fuck. Fuck.

This could start a war between the Boston and New York families. The two families had been at peace for the last fifty years, but things had changed, causing tension between them. It all started when Donovan Muldoon handed over control of the Muldoon family to Sean O'Reilly's new son-in-law, Declan Quinn. The two families had merged, becoming the largest, most powerful family on the East Coast, something Frank Moretti was not happy about. If Moretti thought he could get a leg up on the O'Reillys using Caitlin as leverage, he would do it. Without hesitation.

Caitlin O'Reilly had a target on her back and only Grady to protect her.

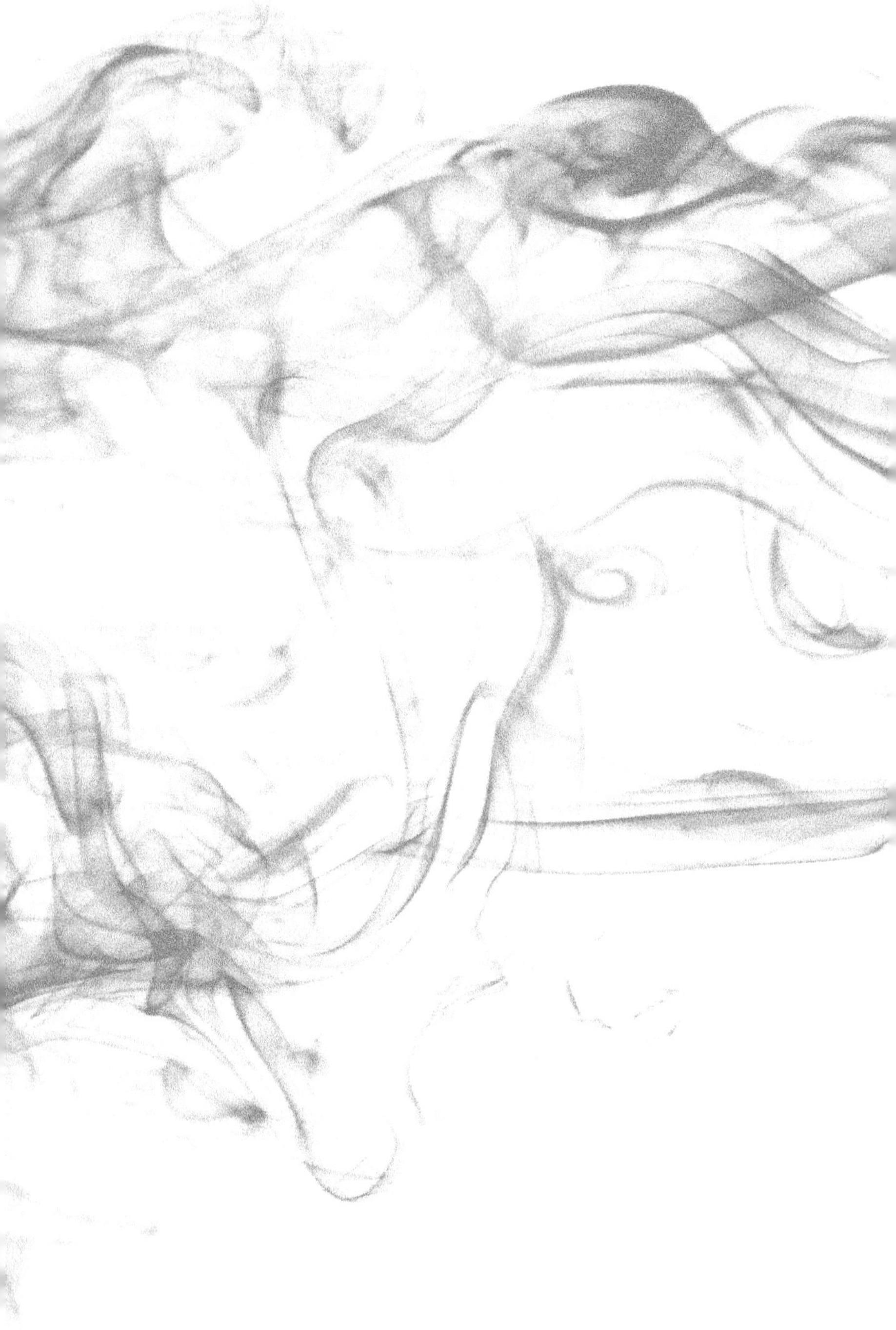

Author Bio

Mimi Francis is a sassy romance writer known for her steamy tales of passion that leave readers breathless. Her creative writing style is filled with vivid imagery and bold characters that make her stories come alive. Born and raised in Montana, Mimi has always had a passion for writing and storytelling.

Mimi's love for writing began when she was a teenager, and she honed her craft by penning countless short stories and journaling. As an adult, she turned to fan fiction as an outlet for her need to write. But it wasn't until she started writing romance novels that she truly found her niche.

When she's not busy crafting her latest heart-pounding romance, Mimi can be found sipping margaritas and indulging in her favorite Marvel movies. She's a self-proclaimed fangirl who can't get enough of superheroes and epic battles. But her true obsession lies with the TV show *Supernatural*, which she has watched from beginning to end more times than she cares to admit.

Mimi is also a wife and mother, as well as a loving dog mom to three adorable Shih Tzus named Sebastian, Sadie, and Sasha. Her furry companions keep her company while she writes and provide endless entertainment with their playful antics.

Mimi's writing career started with her first novel, *Private Lives*, the first book in her *Second Chances in Hollywood* series. Since then, she has published several more books, including the Loves of Lakeside series, set in her home state of Montana. Mimi enjoys writing strong female leads and steamy romance scenes that leave readers wanting more.

> You can connect with Mimi on Instagram and Facebook at @author.mimi.francis, on Twitter at @author_mimi, on TikTok at @authormimifrancis, or on her website mimifrancis.com.

More books from 4 Horsemen Publications

Romance

Ann Shepphird
The War Council

Emily Bunney
All or Nothing
All the Way
All Night Long: Novella
All She Needs
Having it All
All at Once
All Together
All for Her

KT Bond
Back to Life
Back to Love
Back at Last

Lynn Chantale
The Baker's Touch
Blind Secrets

Broken Lens
Blind Fury
Time Bomb
VIP's Revenge
Chef's Taste
The Gold Standard

Mandy Fate
Love Me, Goaltender
Captain of My Heart

Mimi Francis
Private Lives
Private Protection
Private Party
Run Away Home
The Professor
Our Two-Week, One-Night Stand
Can't Fight the Feelings

Discover more at 4HorsemenPublications.com